THE LAST LAUGH

STORIES WHERE WOMEN
TAKE CENTRE-STAGE

The Last Laugh

Stories Where Women
Take Centre-Stage

Gajra Kottary

JAICO PUBLISHING HOUSE

Mumbai Delhi Bangalore Kolkata Hyderabad Chennai Ahmedabad

Published by Jaico Publishing House
121 Mahatma Gandhi Road
Mumbai - 400 023
www.jaicobooks.com

© Gajra Kottary

THE LAST LAUGH
Stories Where Women Take Centre-Stage
ISBN 81-7992-125-5
(Cover Photo Jarita Rayasam)

First Jaico Impression: 2003
Second Jaico Impression: 2003
Third Jaico Impression: 2003

Printed by
Rashmi Printers
31, New Islam Mills Compound, Currey Road (E)
Mumbai - 400 012 • E-mail: tiwarijp@vsnl.net

AUTHOR'S NOTE

Most of my time these days is spent in writing for audiences in darkened halls or in bedrooms. No one really has the grasp of the mindset of these people munching popcorn, much less the ephemeral tastes of TV viewers who have the frightening power of zapping your creation with the press of a finger on their remotes. It is a hard and unforgiving business in which success is solely measured in terms of luring the greatest number of eyeballs to watch your opus. And the indices are box-office returns and TRPs.

Writing a book is much more satisfying. It is a pristine effort unsullied by the pulls and pressures of the world of commerce. The plot unspools itself at an unhurried pace. There are no producers and channel executives ready to tweak my tales, in the belief that they add allure to them. Nor are there directors waiting to give a zing to my characters. The readers too are more forgiving: they will not walk out. And no one zaps a remote.

Even if as an author I still cannot see my readers, I think I am familiar with them. Just as every writer believes that she/he connects with a public; a vast audience which would like a good story. It is a constituency which relates to the narrative, identifies with the characters and empathises with their experiences. In this case, the protagonists in the stories are urban and the settings and sensibilities are Indian.

The Last Laugh was a labour lasting several months. It was shaped through the hours and days snatched from deadlines of the professional and personal kind. The stories in this book, like those in my earlier collection written six years ago, are woven around women.

That is because they hold up half the heavens. If that is not a reason good enough, here is another. Because I find that men are more interested in women than in themselves....

Mumbai
November 2002

ABOUT THE AUTHOR

Gajra Kottary topped the post-graduate course in journalism from the Indian Institute of Mass Communications, New Delhi, and won The Hindu Gold Medal in 1988. After working for a while with *The Statesman* and the Magna group, she quit the profession to raise her children. In 1996 she published her first book of short stories *Fragile Victories*.

She started her scriptwriting career as a script associate with Mahesh Bhatt. Gajra is now writing the story and screenplay of a Hindi film to be directed by Anubhav Sinha and a bilingual production to be directed by Mahesh Manjrekar. She is co-writing the daily *Astitva — Ek Prem Kahani* currently on air directed by Ajai Sinha. Some of the serials Gajra has earlier written are *Hamare Tumhare* and *Panaah*.

Gajra lives in Mumbai with her husband and two children.

DEDICATION

This book is for my children Advait and Aastha
who, many a time, had to forego
little pleasures with their mother
to make this book happen

CONTENTS

CONTENTS

1

All for the Good Cause

All For The Good Cause

In these times when a prosperous urbanite is forty-five, he is not supposed to look a day beyond thirty. And five years ago, when my Abhigyaan was that age he didn't even look twenty-five. I remember watching him fondly from the front door every morning as he got into the backseat of the grey Ambassador at 9:20 sharp to be driven to work. It was the one time in the day that I saw him from far enough to really know how handsome he still looked.

But then that had been the time that he was only MY Abhigyaan. The husband I loved, the father of my children, Maneka and Pranay. He did not yet 'belong to the people' then as he belongs now.

The man that lay before me at this moment was not mine alone. I had to remember and remind myself of that so many times in a day. He did not even look much like the Abhigyaan I knew.

In the last five years, he had aged twenty.

It was not a disease, a calamity, or the excesses of a corrupt lifestyle. None of these. It was due to what he often called 'the turning point in his life' when interviewed by admiring journalists.

Abhigyaan had always been philosophically inclined and had insights into life and its problems like few had. It was a quality that mesmerised all those who came in contact with him. It was a rare person — amongst his half score staff at the ministry that he worked — who had not turned to him for advice at some point or the other in those twelve years that he worked there. And those were the twelve most beautiful years of my life, too.

How beautiful they were, I realised only much after they had long passed. At that time I was often irked at how few of his off-duty hours Abhigyaan had gradually started to spend at home. True, that the children were now old enough to be almost completely on their own. True also that romance in our marriage had somewhat dulled. In fact we had both often talked of how our lives needed refocussing. It was just that I imagined that we'd do this together, as we'd done all the earlier years of 'focussed parenting'.

I thought then that at that time we'd read together, go for long walks, maybe get to know each others' fantasies and perhaps even help them come true. That's what 'refocussing' meant to a woman like me. I did not want to admit or accept that my man was meant for a larger purpose in life. I should have been grateful, that his mid-life crisis did not lead him into the arms of another woman. But, in fact, it led to a fight for justice, for people he had earlier never even had anything to do with.

The tribals of the Teesar district of U P were protesting the cutting down of some of their forests for the making of a road that would help connect the district to all the prominent towns of the state. The state government claimed that it would change their lives for the better. The environmentalists with a handful of tribals were convinced it would be their nemesis.

It was true that studies of the effects of such developmental projects went to show that dispossessed and displaced families never really recovered economically. And so Swami Dhireesh, a social figure of the region was determined this time to give the government a run for its ideas and spearhead a movement to oppose the road plan, tooth and nail.

Abhigyaan was then deputy-secretary in the Public Works Department. Given his ability to deal with and convince people with his oratory he had been pushed forward by the department to deal with the Swami and hopefully win him over to compromise, so that work on the road could begin. I still remember the date. It was 19th July, 1996. Abhigyaan had shared his state of mind with me that morning before he left to meet Swami Dhireesh.

Swami Dhireesh was a man whom he had long admired and hoped to meet, and I knew that there were few men that Abhigyaan actually looked up to. And Abhigyaan admired Swami Dhireesh for being one of the few men who had ceaselessly, and selflessly, worked for the downtrodden in society. Abhigyaan had explained to me that the Swami was so much like the social reformers of previous centuries like Swami Vivekananda and Rabindranath Tagore, for whom the espousal of social causes was as important and perhaps linked to their personal quest for spiritual salvation.

Abhigyaan's anticipation at meeting Swami Dhireesh that morning had however been tempered with the realisation that his mission was to convince him to abandon the campaign to lead the tribals. He shared his divided state of mind with me. And the only way I could help him out would be to counsel him that it would be understandable if he couldn't succeed in his expected line of duty. What would be, would be... and that really was a highly comfortable feeling in public life. Privately, I was sure that Abhigyaan, unable to espouse something that he did not a hundred per cent believe in, would come back with mission unaccomplished. I would never have however dreamt that that would be the day his life's own mission would be found.

Abhigyaan returned in the evening looking preoccupied. I had learnt not to intrude upon him in those initial few hours of his return from the office. He usually opened up much later and on his own. But that day he slept early. The next morning he woke up early too and asked me over our morning cup of tea whether I loved him enough to stand by him through thick and thin for all times to come.

"Of course I do and I will," I had said and he had looked relieved.

I had meant what I had said. But it was much more than I had bargained for. Abhigyaan resigned from his prestigious IAS post that day. The next day he left us all to live life from then on like the tribals whose cause he had completely crossed over to and whose lifestyle he felt he must adopt if he were to truly empathise with them.

A few weeks later, Swami Dhireesh moved back to his headquarters to lend his name to another cause. So Abhigyaan was left alone to become the messiah of the tribals. He moved into the cottage near the Beenwa river where they looked after him as one of their own. Abhigyaan had insisted that Maneka, Pranay and I live in a small flat that he had bought for us a few kilometres away. Money was very tight but Abhigyaan said that that was in a way a good thing, for Maneka and Pranay would now perforce have to toughen up to face life.

Life changed rapidly over the next few months. Abhigyaan locked horns with the very people that he had once worked with. He went on several fasts at various points in the agitation, and that, combined with the legal steps that he took on behalf of the tribals, had succeeded in stalling the road construction now for almost four years. The tribals, their cause and Abhigyaan became international media celebrities and thanks to them Teesar became a tourist spot of Uttar Pradesh.

Everyone told me that I should be proud of Abhigyaan whose selflessness and ideals were now beginning to be compared to those of Gandhi. My Abhigyaan? Were they really talking of him, I often wondered?

It is the fifth day of his fast unto death, and I've been in this tent staring at him in his stupor like state for three days now. Maneka and Pranay have been coming and going but otherwise managing pretty much on their own. Their friends go to parks in the evening and discos at night. But my brave children hold part time jobs and even cook themselves a spartan dinner at night if I am late in returning from the tuition classes that I take. They haven't yet protested too much against this 'toughening up'. Nor have I. It's not easy to do that when the entire nation considers you the family of a national hero.

And the hero lies before me at this moment... his hair coarse and dry. The lips that once transported me to ecstasy, are now chapped and bleeding. The deep warm breath that made me secure all night is now hot, raspy and short but I'm grateful it's there at all. The paunch that Maneka and Pranay used to tease him about has now sunk below his ribs and his skin is stretched somewhat loosely over his bones. All the hundreds of hours I'd spent cleaning and cooking the best of food to nourish his flesh and blood have come to nothing, as the cause has sucked at his very form. And yet it remains unsatisfied.

The doctor told me clearly this morning that Abhigyaan's life now hung just by the slender thread of his will power. And it was only I who knew that that thread might be slender, but unfortunately it was very stubborn!

Yes, I dare to say unfortunately, because it is this very will power that is going to make it difficult for Abhigyaan to give in and end his fast if the state remained firm in its stand favouring the road project. That incidentally, was another truth that the minister had told me three mornings ago, for now that the Supreme Court verdict had ruled in the government's favour, all that they would have to contend with were the emotions of the people and the media and the conviction of Abhigyaan.

The minister had told me that everything was in my hands now. The project would be going full steam ahead anyway, but since the contractors would be happier to work without fear of controversy or revolt they had requested me to convince Abhigyaan to concede so that the tribals would do so too. Privately, they had offered that if Abhigyaan did concede, they would all contribute a percentage of their budget in cash towards any other 'good cause' he might want to fight for.

The contractors had come to me every morning in these last three days and I had honestly pleaded that I had no influence over Abhigyaan's decision to call off his fast and thus make the tribals agree to adjust to the government's alternate plans for them. That was really the truth but it didn't seem so to them. "Bhabhiji surely he'll give in to your wishes if you convince him to," the grey safari suit had said. "Just think about it... we'll come again later."

Abhigyaan opened his eyes slightly. I noticed that his pupils moved involuntarily from side to side along his upper eyelid. I held his warm hand, I noticed that his thumb stuck stubbornly to his palm trying, but failing, to respond to my touch. The doctor had said this was a sign of severe dehydration.

He seemed to be looking at me — if that's what looking could be called without the pupils in place. And I could clearly see our future in the glaze of his blank eyes.

I can see myself sitting in this tiny hut with folded hands as hordes of people float past me whispering words of condolence. Then Pranay and Maneka come to my rescue and take me back to our small home in the town.

Maneka, the girl whom we had once planned to send to Harvard, has given up her studies. Pranay no longer plays football, the game he could once kill for. They are lovely children. Only I am a wretched mother to them.

"Abhigyaan?" I whispered into his ear "They have agreed to everything."

Abhigyaan pressed his hand against mine. I knew he was asking, "Are you sure?"

"Yes, yes Abhigyaan... have I ever told you an untruth."

This time his hand jerked to say, "No, of course I believe you."

"So have this and leave it all to me," I said, lifting the cover from the glass of water kept by his side. I helped him rise slightly and put the glass to his lips. "No, no only a little right now... it must go in slowly," I said even as I watched him clench the rim of the glass with his teeth, his hot breath causing ripples in the water.

"That's enough for now. You rest awhile," I said as I slowly helped him lie down again and then got up to leave the room, looking at him one more time.

The news of Abhigyaan breaking his fast soon spread like wildfire. Within minutes, grey safari suit had come with the bag of contributions from the contractors which he handed over to me to manage and use for the 'good cause' of my choice.

I bid grey safari suit goodbye — warning him to be discreet for a while about what I had accomplished for him. Clutching the bag I peeped into Abhigyaan's room one last time. He was surrounded by his beloved tribals, one of whom was patiently feeding their hero some fruit-juice, teaspoon by teaspoon. His eyes had begun to focus and looked as if they were searching for someone. I knew he would be fine in course of time... but by then his eyes must not find what they searched for.

I turned away and walked out of the hut. Maneka and Pranay were walking towards me, fear writ large on their face.

"How's Papa?" Pranay asked.

"He's going to be fine for he's ended his fast. But we can't see him now, we are leaving for Delhi right now."

"But why?" asked Maneka.

"So that we can live our lives," I said as I turned both of them roughly by their shoulders to ensure that they walk with me, and not towards their father. The nonplussed children did my bidding as I had finally done their's today.

"How can we leave like this Ma? We haven't got anything with us. Let us at least pack our bags at home? We'll need at least a few basic things wherever we go," Maneka spoke again.

"Ma, what's in that bag?" asked Pranay.

"It is for a good cause," I said cryptically.

2

Such a Long Journey

Such a Long Journey

The August Kranti Express was already on the platform at Bombay Central station. Cheerful two-toned cream and orange coloured coaches, with curtains behind the sealed windows of the air-conditioned cabins, colloquially called *dabbas*.

Smita looked at the passenger list outside Coach B. Yes — there was her name : B-9 Mrs Smita Raghavan. Thankfully B-10 was to be occupied by a woman too — Mrs Priya Deshmukh. Whatever anyone might claim, the comfort value of sharing a coach with a woman on a 17-hour journey was much more than with a man — no matter what his age or status might be, thought Smita.

She carried her bag deftly, at waist level, as she walked sideways through the narrow aisle towards her sleeper and settled into it.

B-10 was already occupied by Priya, a woman in her late thirties, who seemed to wear her smartly-cropped, slightly-salt and mostly-pepper hair with quiet dignity. Progressive, but no-nonsense type, would perhaps be the most appropriate words to describe Priya.

Priya looked intently at twenty-seven year old confident and radiant Smita and smiled at her. She then rested her left elbow on her bag as it leaned against the 'wall' and looked out of the window. Smita followed to do the same with her right elbow resting on her bag.

"Anyone else with you?" asked Priya turning away from the window.

"No, no one else. You too... you're travelling alone?" asked Smita.

"Yes, I'm alone too. I'm Priya Deshmukh," said Priya putting her hand out.

"And I'm Smita Raghavan. Hi! It looks like both of us are together 'alone' in this large coupé," said Smita with a chuckle, as she clasped Smita's hand.

"That's the advantage of travelling off-season," said Priya.

"Absolutely. I told my husband Pogy that this was the best time to travel for a woman alone — no rush, no crush. I'm so glad I timed it right," said Smita.

"I too always make sure that I avoid travelling during the holiday season. Of course my nieces and nephews get terribly upset because they're at school half the time that I go on holiday," said Priya.

"It's almost five o'clock now so I don't think anybody else is going to join us. Shall I draw the curtains?" asked Smita.

"Yes, yes go ahead. Then we can stretch out our legs a bit more without getting self-conscious," said Priya with a smile. And she proceeded to do just that, now resting her head on the bag she had earlier leaned on.

As she turned to go back to her seat Smita glanced at Priya's hairy legs that became visible as her saree hitched up to her knees. Thank God she herself didn't wear sarees — for unwaxed legs were among some of the most repulsive sights she could ever imagine.

"Do you live in Delhi or Bombay?" asked Priya as she settled herself a little more comfortably.

"In Delhi," Smita replied. "I came to Bombay last week for a reunion of our school friends. We had a real ball this entire week. You're going to Delhi on a holiday?"

"Yes, I live in Bombay," said Priya.

The guard whistled and the train slowly moved out of the station. Smita exclaimed, "Bon voyage friend."

"Bon voyage to you too," smiled back Priya.

"Now tell me Smita, you're married aren't you?" she said, her eyes focussing on the *mangalsutra* around Smita's neck. "Your husband — he's a nice man I must say, to allow a young pretty wife to go on a week's outstation holiday without him."

It was a rather intimate statement to open a conversation with, thought Smita, a little taken aback before she proceeded to reply.

"Yes, you're right indeed — he's a fantastic husband. In fact he is the one who encouraged me to go. He always tells me never to miss out on any opportunity for a new experience or change," said Smita with a smile as she visualised Pogy's smiling visage.

"You're either a very lucky girl, or else you're just recently married," said Priya with a laugh.

"I don't think four years is too recent, is it? But yes, my husband is a really wonderful person and therefore I think I'm extremely lucky."

"Isn't that the case with you too? I mean, travelling without hubby?" she laughed.

"Well yes, but we travelled away from each other much

before this journey. I'm divorced now. It's been almost six years since. I know I still put Mrs as a prefix to my name, but that's entirely due to reasons of convenience. In fact, I've even reverted to my maiden surname. I live alone and I love it — Bombay is a city that makes it possible," said Priya with a laugh.

"Every year or so I visit my parents, brothers and sisters in Delhi for a few days. That's about enough of a family scene that I can take at this stage of my life. Whenever I'm in Delhi for a little longer than a week, I yearn to come back to Bombay and be by myself again. It's been like this for a long time now," said Priya.

"It must have become like this after your divorce I think. Otherwise few women would really choose to be alone. Divorce always makes one bitter and leaves one with a whole lot of pain and a feeling of defeat. I've seen these things happen really close, for my husband Pogy had been through a divorce much before we got married. I know about the entire gamut of feelings that a divorcee goes through," said Smita.

"Pogy's divorce left him withdrawn and alone — it must have been the same with you too," said Smita, now realising that perhaps she had got too carried away with her own thoughts. It was now she who had perhaps unwittingly steered the conversation onto very intimate territory.

But Priya took it well. She smiled back at Smita. Thank God, Smita thought to herself that she had taken her words in the right context.

"You're an intelligent woman, Smita," said Priya. "What you've said is really the plain truth. After a divorce, it takes a long time to work the bitterness out of one's system. First the loneliness crushes you, but after some time it becomes a companion," said Priya, her eyes shifting focus from Smita's face to a vacant space on the ceiling, clearly chary of meeting Smita's eyes just yet.

"It's more difficult to get rid of the fear and bitterness if one is alone. It's easier when someone is there to help pull you out of the morass. I had to work on Pogy for quite sometime before he was able to get back his faith in love and life again. But four years of marriage later, I must say that it's been worth every minute," said Smita fondly.

"A second chance in love, happens much more easily to a man than a woman. Women by nature are more cynical than men. And another big irony is that it's only after a woman loses her partner — it's only then that she starts discovering herself as an individual," said Priya.

"Did that happen to you too?" asked Smita.

"Yes it did. He was such a double-faced person. We were equals who were in the same class in college when we fell in love. But after marriage the whole equation changed. He didn't like me going out— not even to work. He was very insecure. He treated me like a maid in the house."

"I took it all in the name of love. But when his eyes started to wander despite me fulfilling his demand of paying him and the home full attention, I decided that it was not worth it after all. Even after all the crushing of my soul, my marriage had proved to be a farce. So I thought I might as well salvage my soul. It was horribly painful doing it after five years of investment in my marriage. But when I think in retrospect today, I'm glad I had the nerve to do it when I did. If I had waited any longer I might not have been able to do it. For one's resolves and strength do diminish with age," said Priya in a subdued tone. "It was tough but I was able to put the marriage totally behind me."

"You're so right Priya. In our country it usually takes a divorce or widowhood, for a woman to start thinking of her own identity. Even a decade ago things were more or less like that. But you know times are changing. More importantly, I think men are changing. They are finally beginning to realise that true happiness in a marriage depends on the woman's development as a person in her own right. She is not just meant to be an appendage to him," said Smita, the optimism of the state of her own life shining through in the conviction with which she spoke her words.

"Do you know Pogy himself didn't want me to change my surname. He said it wasn't fair to me, nor to the family that had brought me up with such love and affection. He's so sweet!" said Smita.

"Maybe you're right. Maybe men are changing — excruciatingly slowly though, but it's finally happening at least in your time. Good for you," said Priya.

"Yes, but it's women like you who've come about half a generation before us who have helped it to happen. All of you, who have paid a heavy personal price for your beliefs, have made men in general change for the better.

" I never really looked upon myself as a social reformer, but hey.... your analysis does make me feel good, I'll confess," said Priya bemused.

"My stand for example, was one that I took merely for selfish or rather self-respecting reasons," said Priya. "I, for one, did it to get out of this syndrome of my husband first, restricting my opportunities for growth in the name of homemaking, and then making me feel inferior. Inferior to the women-of-the world with whom he got into one affair after another. I stood up for myself, to prevent myself being degraded to a stage where I started to think of myself as a worthless human being," said Priya.

"That's precisely what I mean Priya. It is principled stands like these that have made men of today realise the importance of treating their women with the dignity that they deserve," said Smita.

"Look at Pogy, for example. To be frank I was ready to forget my own ambitions and talents. I'm personally too laid back to make the effort to do anything of consequence with my life. But Pogy keeps pushing me out of my laziness to do something worthwhile. He says it's good for my sense of self-worth and for our happiness as a couple, that I grow as an individual. He's proved to be right — today my ceramics business is booming — and my success makes me feel so much more fulfilled as a person. It's all due to his encouragement," continued a beaming Smita.

"You're really lucky to have a husband like that. He's poles apart from my husband — I mean my ex-husband, when he used to be my husband that is," laughed Priya.

"You know Priya, at this reunion we had in Bombay I was telling all my friends about Pogy. At first they kept teasing me about having been wise enough to have chosen to become an old man's darling rather than a young man's slave — something that most of them seem to have done. You see there is an almost twelve year difference between Pogy and me. But after they had all finished with the ragging, they admitted that they all secretly envied me — they all said that I'm one lucky woman. Pogy has really proved to be a fantastic husband in the whole world," said Smita, her eyes shut tight as if to emphasise the sincerity of her statement.

"Some people do have all the luck ! What I yearned for, you got so easily — but then that's the way of the world. Isn't this the reason that makes the most independent and individualistic of us believe in the theory of karma?" asked Priya with a calm smile.

"Yes it sure does," said Smita. "I too have begun to believe in it, of late."

"B-9, B-10, dinner is ready," shouted the train attendant sliding open the door brusquely.

Priya got up with a start, covering her hairy legs as she pursed her lips, taken aback and irritated at this sudden intrusion.

Smita however had by now got up like a bolt from the blue rexine seat and quickly taken the two trays from the attendant. She had sensed Priya's discomfiture.

"There's no point expecting etiquette from them. It's just too much for their class of people," said Smita with a frown on her face as she handed a tray to Priya.

"Thanks," said Priya "both for the tray and your alertness — for I did get very fazed with the attendant's sudden entry."

"No problem," said Smita as she settled herself next to Priya and they started to eat.

"The food has improved since I last travelled. At least the *pulao* tastes like pea and not kerosene *pulao*," said Priya, tucking it in with relish.

"You like the *pulao*? Why don't you take some of mine too. I'm off rice since the last two weeks."

"Must be to do with weight-management isn't it? You're slim enough already," said Priya.

"Well frankly yes — it is," said Smita as she scooped out her rice and served it on Priya's tray.

"I'm sure Pogy likes you slim-n-svelte. Men sometimes don't

say it openly but they don't like wives when they put on weight. Mine used to make such cutting remarks! Thank God at least now I can eat what I want," said Priya enjoying her *pulao* with gusto.

"Actually Pogy doesn't hassle me about it — he says he'll always like me however I look. But I myself get unnerved at the prospect of putting on weight," said Smita.

"Hmmm," said Priya thoughtfully as the two of them went on to complete the meal in silence.

Silence that was just as comfortable as their conversation had been a few minutes ago. As was their sleep all through the night, gently rocked by the movement of the train as though they were babies in their cradles. Smita was amused by the sight and sound of Priya's snoring through the night. She seemed to have lost all her feminine qualities, along with the man in her life!

In the morning Priya looked on indulgently as she saw Smita carefully making up her face and dabbing on perfume — obviously excited at the thought of meeting Pogy at the station. Later they exchanged contact numbers and addresses in Delhi, promising to meet again. And they both knew that each of them really meant what they said about wanting to keep up the association that had started with this journey.

.

It was 9:40 a.m. as the train slowly trundled into New Delhi railway station. Smita pulled Priya's hand and led her near the door of the coach where they both waited for the train to come to a complete halt.

"You've got to meet my Pogy. In fact, if no one comes for you, you'll come with us. East of Kailash you said you had to go, didn't you?" she asked.

"No no, I'll manage. I've always managed. I'll definitely meet your New Age Man but no dropping *ka chakkar* today. I'll go on my own," said Priya.

"Okay okay, we'll see. But at least come with me right now. Yipee! There he is.... can you see him.... The one in the pin-striped blue shirt!" squealed Smita as she pointed her finger at the crowd.

Priya could not make him out, as the train swept past a sea of faces, each of them bobbing their heads concernedly from left to right to identify the coach from which their loved ones would alight.

Smita hopped down from the steps running energetically ahead, while Priya followed, hesitant and reticent to intrude upon this very private moment when Smita was going to be united with Pogy. She unabashedly hugged the man in a pin striped shirt, with a salt and pepper mop of hair, who then broke free to stare at Priya.

"Priya this is Pogy, Pogy this is Priya. Pogy. Priya and I have just been together on this short journey but it feels like we've known each other for ages," said Smita failing to notice the hard stare that Pogy was giving Priya. Then she turned to Priya, who had been looking just as stony-eyed at Pogy.

"How have you been Priya?" asked Pogy softly.

"I'm all right. But you've certainly come a long way with Smita — I see," said Priya, as she turned to a non-plussed Smita.

"It's been a really long journey for all of us. Especially for him — from my Pratap to your Pogy. It's time now, to say goodbye. Goodbye Smita and God bless you," said Priya finally, as she walked away slowly with her bags.

3

Happily Ever After

Happily Ever After

What a fantastic way to begin the last working day of the week. Sreela read the letter that had been right on top of the pile in her mail tray for the sixth time in the last ten minutes.

The Morning Post
The Post Building
Fifth Avenue
New York – 10022
USA

Dear Ms. Dixit,

Congratulations! You have been unanimously chosen by our jury for one of our annual journalistic awards. You have been found to be the most worthy candidate for this year's Best Asian Social Journalist award.

As you might be already aware, your choice for being conferred this award had been prompted by the overwhelming response — both national and international — to your coverage of the Kundabai story last year.

We shall be informing you very shortly about the details of the awards ceremony next month, along with your travel arrangements. But to proceed any further in this matter, we would require from you as early as possible the following: A formal letter of your acceptance of this award, a copy of your resumé with some of your recent pictures and, most importantly, 2-3 recent "happily ever after" pictures of Kundabai to whose life you made all the difference.

Awaiting your response.

Thanking you,
Yours sincerely,

Whitney Brown
Associate Editor - The Morning Post.

Sreela's little cabin was soon teeming with people. Her effusive colleagues, some smiling genuinely, others pretending to do so, shiny-eyed secretaries and even a couple of genuflecting juniors. All morning long Sreela smiled until her jaws ached. Then, her editor Pranay Bose who flew in from Calcutta at noon, called her right away into his cabin.

Pranay Bose was so proud of her. Especially proud, because he was the one who had given her a job in the first place. He had chosen her over several of the better qualified mass communication post-graduates nearly five years ago. The reason as he had told her had been her fighting spirit, an opinion on everything and a zeal to change the world. She had been told that though she was short on objectivity, she made up for it by being strong on rhetoric and was therefore such a refreshing change from the 'trained to write well' graduates of journalism schools.

"I can afford only one Sreela in an editorial staff of ten.... But one Sreela is certainly more interesting than all the nine put together," Pranay had often stated to his colleagues after a couple of drinks at the Press Club. He had also been very effusive in his compliments to her, in private to begin with. In course of time, however, he had started to express his admiration of Sreela much more openly.

"Sreela, you have really done me proud," he had said after one of her first stories had been publicly lauded. "Maybe, thanks to you, we shall see the return of the activist type of journalism that had been such a vital part of our lives in the eighties," he had said with a nostalgic look in his eyes.

Sreela had certainly risen rapidly above the ranks of regular journalists who just did the usual reportage. She consistently wrote stories that had triggered off changes in her subjects' lives and had proved, time and again, that if like-minded people joined hands to fight for justice, it was possible for individuals to get it.

Sreela's first such story had been published four years ago. It had been a dramatic expose of the case of a poor twelve year old girl, Salma, who had been 'married' to an Arab in exchange for a few goodies for her poor parents. Thanks to the hue and cry and enquiries that had followed, the Arab had gone underground, hopefully chastened forever. Salma was now in a girl's hostel of an English medium school, her education having been taken over by a public fund set up by Pranay Bose's newspaper.

Pranay Bose had been proud of all of Sreela's stories. Each one of the seven that had followed Salma's. Today his faith in her seemed vindicated when a prestigious international newspaper like *The Morning Post* had chosen to confer an award on Sreela.

It was therefore understandable that Pranay Bose just couldn't stop shaking her hand today as she faced him in his cabin. "I'm so proud of you," he said again and again, his eyes transfixed on the letter lying under the paper weight on his table. "You must send them your acceptance letter and the documents right away."

"There's a problem Sir," said Sreela, disengaging her hand from his with some relief to pick up the letter and point it out to him, when she could well have told him about it instead. "It says here that they require from me, a recent 'happily ever after' kind of picture of Kundabai. I don't have one with me right now, Sir. For that I'll have to travel to Manmad again."

"So go Sreela. Go today itself.... It's the beginning of the weekend tomorrow. You can easily get the pictures by tomorrow and come back in time to post your stuff to the US by Monday morning. Consider your leave sanctioned and the office car at your disposal, all your travel expenses are granted. You can take an advance right away. Anything for you my dear girl, after all you have done our newspaper very

very proud," said Bose breathlessly.

Sreela was an expert at travelling at short notice. She slung her camera around her neck then satisfactorily examined the pair of keds she always kept at the office. They'd always stood by her in good stead when she had to traverse the unfriendly roads surrounding Bombay.

She thought a little about her clothes. Frankly, it would be more convenient to buy a set of undergarments and a T-shirt to go with her jeans, from the department store below the office, than waste a couple of hours going back home into the suburbs to pick them up! That decided it.

Before she knew it, Sreela was sitting in the backseat of the office car, thankfully out of mean Bombay and onto broader and faster roads on a day of light traffic.

The practical and organised Sreela usually used her time on the way to an assignment in mentally preparing for it. It was important to frame the right questions, arguments and counter arguments in possibly-changing scenarios. But this time it was refreshingly different. She could afford to empty her mind of all such burdens, and she could afford to revel in a sense of achievement at the positive change that she had brought about in someone's life. One for which she was about to be internationally acclaimed.

Sreela took out the picture of Kundabai that she had clicked one year ago. Emaciated, but beautiful, Kundabai sitting cross-legged but determined outside the hut of her lover Vilas Kondke, staring with large sunken eyes at the tiny bundle of a baby in her lap.

"I really loved him. I really believed him when he said he loved me... that's the only reason I gave in to him. But now he refuses to marry me.... Tell me memsahib is this not his child and I, his child's mother, for him to want to shirk taking our responsibility. But memsahib, I will not quietly accept my fate like other women... I will sit here on a dharna until he takes us both into his home," she had said. "Till then my house is here... on a bamboo mat under the open sky," Kundabai had said resolutely.

What a poignant picture it had made! And the way Sreela had captured and projected her grit along with the four articles she wrote on her one after another, had resulted in a national, and then international, sympathy wave for Kundabai.

Hundreds of people had sent Kundabai financial aid, which she had proudly returned. Several villagers had been shamed enough by her story and offered to rehabilitate her. Rajaram, the old rich and ugly moneylender of Manmad village, had even offered to marry her promising to treat her well all his life. He had said that he wanted to give her so much happiness that she'd forget that Vilas Kondke had ever happened. But the righteous Kundabai had scornfully refused. "My happiness lies in my acceptance by the father of my child and the man I loved," Kundabai had said, with steely determination.

Kundabai's cause became a cause célèbre and had in course of time made the village elders impress upon Vilas to make amends. Within a week, a shame-faced Vilas Kondke had taken Kundabai and their daughter in. Sreela's mission had been accomplished.

"I think this is the house of that husband of her's," said her driver Kader. He was usually right in his sense of direction and moreover he had been constantly with her all through last year's campaign.

"No, Kundabai does not stay in this house now," said a voice. "Kundabai lives there in that pucca house," said a little girl wearing a muddied grey school uniform, the large red ribbons on her two tightly braided oiled plaits bouncing as she played hopskotch. She pointed to a one-storeyed house at the corner of the lane, brightly painted in pink.

Sreela asked Kader to park the car there. "Nice house," he commented. "Looks like Kundabai and Vilas are doing well for themselves."

Sreela could sense the trace of envy in Kader's voice at this apparent prosperity of those who for him were really 'people-like-us.' But she herself felt happy and in some measure responsible for this turnabout.

Sreela walked across the road to the pretty pink house and savoured its surroundings. It would surely make a pretty picture for the foreign papers. All the signs of a happy Indian home in the country — one that SHE had helped make happy.

Sreela focussed her camera and adjusted it to include the pretty Rangoli design in front of the blue wooden door in the frame. The plastic *toran* leaves at the top of the door — each of which had an image of a different Hindu God painted in gold on it — flapped in the warm dry breeze of the early evening. Satisfied with the picture she'd taken Sreela proceeded to knock on the door.

The door opened, only as much as the safety chain would allow it to. Enough however to make clearly visible the smiling face of Kundabai. Her face lit up the moment that she saw Sreela. She removed the safety chain quickly and opened the door to hug her. Sreela felt Kundabai sweating profusely beneath the heavy silk saree she was wearing. She had filled out everywhere and was almost unrecognisable, her belly clearly heavy with child. Her face was oily and shining, her maang filled with orange sindoor from forehead to the back of her head. Kundabai was resplendent in the glow of a happy marriage and second time motherhood. The haunted look that Sreela associated her with had gone forever.

Kundabai plied Sreela with country goodies, *puran poli*, *modak*, *chakli* and much else, refusing to accept her protests. Eventually Sreela virtually begged her to understand that more than food, what she really needed was to click a happy picture of Kundabai and her family.

Kundabai finally did understand. She smiled and called out to a maid servant. The maid brought in Kundabai's one-year old to sit on her lap, cautioning the nonplussed child not to kick Amma — for it would hurt her little sibling in Amma's stomach.

"But I need Vilas to pose with all of you," Sreela explained. "Where's he?"

Kundabai's face fell. "He's not my husband anymore," she said.

"I was wrong Memsahib, absolutely wrong. You all helped me... you made him take us back and fulfill his responsibilities. He did he gave us a roof over our head, food, water, money, status everything that he could afford. But he couldn't love us anymore. And I realised soon enough that I couldn't live without his love."

"So did he leave you and...." Sreela asked hoarsely.

"No memsahib... I left him. I was the one who had chained him. And it was i who set him free too. And then I set myself free too."

"But this house? And the child that you're expecting...."

"Rajaram's... I married Rajaram."

"The old moneylender who had said that he loved you,"

Sreela cried out in horror biting her tongue to avoid using the word 'ugly' to describe him in these new changed circumstances.

"At least he's not a liar. He didn't just say it... he really does love me... I've experienced true love, comfort and enough happiness for a lifetime in this one year, memsahib. You take your picture memsahib.... It is a happy family picture you require isn't it? A happily-ever-after picture? My face will not lie and nor will I memsahib. Not now, not ever again."

Sreela stood up slowly and walked away from Kundabai. She was feeling faint. She realised the award which she had won had just slipped from her grasp. That was how the cookie had crumbled.

Sreela turned around and stopped at an optimum distance of about twelve feet, and then aimed and clicked. A truly happily-ever-after picture.

◈ ◈ ◈

4

The Guru

The Guru

Indu looked at the contents of her carrybag again. Two sarees, one nightgown, undergarments, three frocks for Aditi and lots of nappies. And right at the bottom of the bag, her beloved pair of ghunghroos.

Would the clothes suffice? She was not really sure. Unlike travellers who pack their bags keeping in mind the duration of the journey and their destination—at this point of time she was not certain of either. The bag and its contents were merely indicative of her decision to break away.

Indu picked up a sleeping Aditi and clutched her handbag with one hand while she held the carrybag with the other. She looked around the bedroom that had been hers and Amitabh's in these last two years and tried to feel nostalgic. For a few brief seconds she succeeded in this too, when her eyes fell upon the twin-frame picture beside their bed. On the left was the picture of their wedding day. Amitabh was looking at her with an amused expression on his face through the flowers of his *sehra* as if to say 'grin and bear it for just a little while more.'

Amitabh had really loved her. She knew that he still did. But it was time that he learnt that she had been grinning and bearing it for far too long now. And her leaving the house today was an ultimatum for him to either learn to stand up to his parents or lose her altogether. Reminded afresh of the need for the firm step that she was taking today Indu looked away from this photograph, even though she could still not resist looking at the one on the right side.

It was the photograph that Amitabh had taken of a tired looking Indu cradling one-day old Aditi at the hospital. Indu put down her carrybag for a moment, removed the photograph from the frame and put it in her handbag. This was a statement that she was making to Amitabh, who would hopefully understand how she was feeling when he would see it missing that evening.

Indu looked at the clock. It was 11 o'clock and she realised that she had better leave soon, or else her mother-in-law would return from the market and her plan would be thwarted.

Indu slowly walked out of the house, and as its familiar grey front gate shut with a clank, for a moment her heart sank. She was doing this to teach Amitabh a lesson — but what if her plan backfired?

What if instead of reforming, Amitabh simply gave up on her and refused to woo her back to the independent home that he had been promising for so long?

Indu steeled herself once again. If that was what was going to be, so be it. Better for her to cope with harsh reality than harbour any more illusions.

She hailed a taxi. Kalanagri, she told him as she first kept her carrybag on the backseat and then settled gently into it so as not to disturb Aditi.

Kalanagri was the housing complex where her guru lived. She had been there only once earlier for a short while, when he had invited them all for the *grihapravesh* of his house. Indu remembered that day almost four years ago very well. At that time she had been introduced to all those present as Guruji's 'star-pupil' — one for whom he said he had great dreams and hopes. That had been such a happy and auspicious occasion, so different from today.

But where else could she possibly go in this condition, in this big bad city? Apart from her marital home, the only place Indu knew fairly well in the entire city of Delhi, was the hostel of the Odissi Kendra where she had spent five wonderful years of her life. She had come there after fighting a minor battle with her parents in their Moradabad home, and had finally been allowed to come to Delhi to pursue her training in Odissi dance. And it was for this reason itself that there was no question of now going back to her parents. Too many years and too much distance had passed between them.

She had no links with the Odissi Kendra either. The only link left with the place and with dance itself, which had once been her lifeline, was Guruji.

Guru Manna Lal was a temperamental guru. A senior teacher at the Kendra, he was always spoken about reverentially by critics and students of Odissi alike.

Guruji himself had learnt dance in the most pristine and strict codes of the guru-shishya *parampara*. But as a concession to modern times and urban living, he had chosen to teach just a handful of students at the Odissi Kendra, run with the patronage of the illustrious industrial group of the Laljis.

Indu had been lucky that Guruji had chosen to teach her. It was not a question of him sensing potential in a candidate alone — theories abounded why he turned away many, extremely talented candidates who came hopefully to the Odissi Kendra year after year for admission. It was said that he looked for a certain combination of *shraddha* (humility) and *dhairya* (staying power) in a student that was sometimes inconsistent with talent itself. And he had obviously found that in Indu.

Indu's eyes brimmed over at the thought of the fatherly

love that she had so often seen in Guruji's eyes. She remembered his caress on her hair as he had blessed her when she had taken Amitabh to meet him, and introduced him as the man she wanted to marry, nearly three years ago.

A few days later Guruji had sat her down after class. "Beti — I have taught you like my own daughter. And you have also done the kind of sadhana that I would expect from a good daughter of mine," he had said.

In the pale shaft of the setting sun in the dance room that evening, he had looked old and tired. "I have many hopes from you, and I wish you marital happiness as I would my own daughter. But through the decades of my experience I have observed that once a girl gets married, she can no longer pursue dance or any other art, with the same passion and devotion as before. There simply isn't enough encouragement and support from the family," he had said with a sigh.

"Now that is a very frustrating situation for both the guru and the shishya. If you have really felt that dance is a part of your life itself, it is not something that you'll be happy giving up. I'm concerned for you beti. How are you going to reconcile dance with your grihastha life? You're a woman after all," Guruji had asked with concern.

Indu remembered how she had proceeded to reassure Guruji about his concerns for her at that time. She herself had been completely assured on that front. And that was because Amitabh, who had been attracted to her in no small measure due to her dance, had promised her all his support and encouragement to continue to pursue dance. She had often told him seriously that dance was both her dharma and her karma in this life even more than being a wife and mother was, and he had always assured her happily that it would remain so.

How wrong she had been! Dance and art, *sadhana* and *riyaz* — they simply meant nothing to Amitabh's parents, and as it was now apparent, to Amitabh too. For Amitabh felt guilty at having gone against his parent's wishes by marrying a girl of his choice. He was therefore ever ready to give her dreams a backseat, in order not to upset them any more than they already were.

Indu was therefore requested to first ingratiate herself with them before she could get her way. Sooner or later they would 'melt' and then all would be completely well again, Amitabh had told her reassuringly. Till then she had to try to be a good and 'normal' sort of *bahu*. This involved doing the regular chores and participating in all the rituals that were part and parcel of an Indian joint family. But now, even two years down the line, Indu's mother-in-law showed no signs of melting.

In fact with Aditi's birth, even Indu's attendance of dance practice sessions at the Kendra, which had been coldly accepted earlier, were frowned upon. *"Bachchi ko chod, ma nachne jati hai,"* her mother-in-law had complained to Amitabh and as always he had requested Indu to toe the line of compliance. Little did he realise, that by asking her to stop dancing, he was crushing her very spirit.

It was a mistake to have married Amitabh. How right Guruji had been in his concerns! thought Indu. And, therefore, it was only at his feet that Indu could hope to start her life afresh. With or without Amitabh, but certainly with dance. These last few months without dance had made Indu clearly realise what was more central to her existence.

But now as Gururani — whose feet she reverentially touched when she entered their home — led her inside, Indu was suddenly afraid. Bereft of the festivities that she had earlier witnessed in this house, there was a strange stillness in the air now, that made her feel alone and dwarfed.

Guruji sat on a diwan in his *riyaz* room. On the wall right behind him was a mammoth black and white picture of him in a meditative dance *mudra*, so huge that it dwarfed his presence.

Guruji looked surprised to see her. Then, as his eyes fell upon the carrybag that she was holding, he sensed that all was not well.

Indu put the bag down and while still holding Aditi, bent down gingerly to touch his feet.

"Jeeti raho," he muttered. Indu felt a trifle embarrassed looking directly at Guruji who looked so different in his lungi and vest, from his usual attire of the Kurta-pyjama that he always wore to class.

Indu sat a few yards away on the cold marble floor and cradled the still-sleeping Aditi across her crossed legs. She began to search for the right words to explain her predicament. But Guruji lifted his hand in a gesture to stop her from doing so.

"I have had years of experience not only in dance, but also in life and people itself. *Ye baal dhoop mein safed nahin hue,*" he said.

"I can see that you have reached a crossroad in your life and have to decide which direction to take. You can take shelter in my house until you have made your decision," he assured. "You must abide by all the rules of this home while you're here."

Just then Gururani entered the room, her head covered with the pallu of her starched pale blue cotton saree. The soft tinkle of the bunch of keys that hung at her waist accompanied her as she walked towards him with his thali of food.

She placed the thali on the floor for a moment and then began to search the room for the floor-stool on which to place it in front of him. She found it a few moments later and placed it in front of Guruji on the diwan. Then she placed his thali on it.

Guruji thundered angrily, "In all these twenty-five years you have still not learnt to place the stool before me, before you get the thali from the *rasoi*. You know this ruins my mood even before I start my meal and yet you will never improve your ways," he said as he glared at Gururani.

Gururani cringed with embarrassment and muttered softly, *"Bhool ho gayee,"* and avoiding Indu's eyes she made an exit. As he saw her leave Guruji nodded his head from side to side. *"Aurat zaat ko bhagwan ne chunkar dheeth banaya hai.* They will just never improve," he stated, nodding his head from side to side.

Gururani entered the room again with a freshly baked puffed *phulka* on the plate, and offered it to Guruji.

"Can you not see that it will take me some time to finish the one on my thali? Why are you dancing on my head like this? Is it such a chore feeding me that you want it over and done with as soon as possible?"

"I thought you might have finished the first one, sometimes you do eat it fast .... I'll take this back and get the next one," Gururani muttered apologetically as she walked out of the room.

Indu watched the scene, trying not to show any reaction as she watched Gururani make a dozen entries and exits through that one meal that she watched Guruji eat. At last he finished eating, and as Guruji burped when Gururani took the thali away, Indu caught a look of blissful relief on Gururani's face.

"It's time for my afternoon nap now," he declared to Gururani. "Take care of the girl and see that she is comfortable in every way."

Gururani dutifully settled Indu and Aditi into the room that belonged to their college-going son Rahul. Rahul had gone to spend a week with his maternal grandparents and was due to return two days later. Gururani told Indu that for these next two days the room was hers to use. After that when Rahul was back, she would make some other arrangement for her if it was needed, she added kindly. Indu merely nodded.

Indu soon realised that Gururani was ever so gracious and maternal. She marvelled the fact that Gururani's face never registered any look of hurt brought about by Guruji's insults and wondered about it. As the latter served Indu her lunch and fed Aditi with the same affection as her grandmother would have, she couldn't help broaching the subject.

"Your Guruji is worshipped by the whole world. But it is I who have the privilege of keeping his home and heart. His insults are a small price I have to pay for this privilege," she explained to Indu softly.

Indu looked up from the food that she was eating. Though it was Guruji who was her link with Gururani, at this moment she felt closer to Gururani than to him.

"He depends on me for all his needs. He's like a child," Gururani said smiling proudly.

"But even a woman has needs and aspirations of her own. Don't you think a man should appreciate and fulfill them in the same manner that he expects her to do so?" Indu questioned, thinking of her own life.

"A woman has to forget her needs and aspirations when she

gets married. They can never ever be fulfilled the way a man's can be," sighed Gururani, as she cajoled Aditi into eating the last morsel of the *dal-bhaat* mix that she had made specially for her.

"It is better to come to terms with the situation and at least enjoy keeping a beautiful and happy home," said Gururani. Then she wiped with the back of her hand, the few specks of food that remained on the table, before she proceeded to the kitchen to wash up.

Gururani had insisted on serving Indu and feeding Aditi first, before eating herself. "It is the dharma of the woman of the house to eat last," she had said righteously.

It was now Indu's turn to serve Gururani, and in the best of Indian tradition, to cajole her into eating more generous helpings. She did it with a feeling of belonging even though she knew that this was not her own home.

Gururani smiled at her. "It feels nice to be served," she said. "All I ever remember after being married is cooking and serving." Then almost as if she were afraid that Indu might get a wrong impression of her state of satisfaction, she hastily added, "but of course, *yehi to ek suhagan ka dharam hai,*"

"Has Guruji never eaten with you?" Indu could not help asking, though she knew it was too personal a question.

"No, never," Gururani replied. "But I don't mind that. He doesn't have to eat with me or express his affection for me publicly, to show that he cares for me. I just know that he does. He has always cared for me. And me? I have always loved him — ever since I can remember," she said shyly.

Indu stared at Gururani's bright red tikka, and the saffron coloured sindoor at the beginning of the maang on her forehead. She thought to herself that Gururani must still be completely awestruck with Guruji. She was so grateful for being married to Guruji. And Guruji must be tolerating her to make the best of the situation he must have been forcibly placed in.

Indu could certainly not imagine Gururani being a creative soulmate to Guruji. No wonder he treated her the way he did — he must be finding it difficult to connect with her. Perhaps in small measure in the same way that she found it difficult to relate to Amitabh anymore. Gururani and Amitabh — they were both made of a similar mettle — with no urges towards art and creativity, despite being married to people for whom these were the very life forces.

Gururani stared at Indu almost as if she had read her thoughts. "I'd like to tell you something beti, *bura mat maanna*. It's not as if I resent giving you shelter here — but I would like to give you a piece of advice. You're a married woman and a mother now — don't stretch your luck too far. If your husband treats you and your child well, don't leave him merely for some vague artistic pursuit. Ultimately a home is much more important for a woman's life and security than any artistic pursuit," she advised.

Indu nodded her head in agreement. She did not want to argue or hurt Gururani. After all, what Gururani had said was probably right from her own narrow point of view. The point of view of a woman, who though married to an artist had probably never experienced magical moments of aesthetic thrill or creative flight.

Gururani had finished eating and urged Indu to take Aditi with her to Rahul's room and make sure to keep her quiet for the next two hours. "Guruji likes absolute silence in the afternoon while he is taking a nap. I take care to remove my footwear when I walk around at this time, lest the sound of my footsteps disturbs him," she explained. "He gets very irritable if his afternoon nap is disturbed."

Indu nodded her head, amused at Gururani's constant reference to her husband as 'Guruji', as she led Aditi to Rahul's room. She noticed Guruji's trophies and pictures all along the walls of the passage that led to Rahul's room. It seemed as if no one else but Guruji lived in this house.

The next two hours passed uneventfully. At five o'clock Guruji emerged, dressed in his kurta-pyjama. He was fresh from his evening bath and looked more the picture of dignity that she had always associated him with. He was soon joined by two of his disciples and prepared to leave to inaugurate the Hiralal Natya Sammelan that was to start that day in the suburbs.

Indu watched as Gururani fussed over him — choosing the appropriate attar for him to wear for the occasion, handing him his kerchief and wiping his Jaipuri *jootis* to gleaming perfection. She saw Gururani watch with indulgence as he slid his feet into the *jootis* and bid them both goodbye.

Gururani shut the door after him. In that instant, like a caged bird suddenly set free, Indu saw Gururani transform. She beckoned Indu to join her as she stretched her legs out on the diwan and blissfully chewed on the paan from Guruji's *paandaan*.

"You don't usually go out with Guruji?" asked Indu.

"He doesn't ask me to go with him, and frankly that's all right with me. I can enjoy some time of relaxation when he is away. Besides, I have to get his meal ready to be served the way he likes it when he returns, and if I go with him that's just not possible," she reasoned. Suddenly Gururani sprang up from the diwan.

"I've never seen you dance Indu. Guruji says you are a very

good dancer. Why don't you dance for me... I have about an hour before I start my work in the kitchen," she said.

Indu looked at Gururani with confusion. In a sense, the thought was tempting. She would be more comfortable initially doing her steps in front of the non-judgmental Gururani, than Guruji, who she was scared might judge her out-of-practice performance too strictly. And she was sure that if she stayed on in their house any longer, he would very soon want her to dance in order to assess her current standard.

"I'd love to Gururani, but.... without Guruji's accompaniment or the tape of his singing....., " said Indu hesitantly.

"What am I here for? I'll sing for you. *Chalo jugalbandi ho jaye,*" smiled Gururani.

"*Aap...?*" stuttered Indu. Surely Gururani knew nothing about dance, leave alone accompaniment, which was the forte of veteran gurus of dance. A non-creative, non-artistic woman....... Surely, Gururani was playing an asinine joke on Indu.

But Gururani would have none of it. She rushed into her room and brought out a pair of ghunghroos for Indu.

"Mine," she said, "from the days that I used to learn dance from Guruji at Natyakshetra," she continued, as she handed them over to Indu.

A bewildered Indu began to tie the ghunghroos on her ankles as Gururani continued reminiscing. "How much I fought with my family to go there..... They did not speak to me for the five years that I was there....... It was only after I was married and Rahul was born that....., " she trailed.

"I don't really blame my family, what would they understand

of art and my urges...," she sighed.

"Maybe they would not. But what about Guruji....?" asked, a shocked Indu.

Gururani gave Indu a piercing stare. Then, in the next instant as though embarrassed at doing so she looked away.

A perplexed Indu muttered. "I'm sorry..... I didn't mean too...."

But Gururani had not heard her. For even before Indu could complete her sentence she saw Gururani shut her eyes in deep concentration as she dwelled on the *sama*.

"Sa....," she sang, perfectly on note, and it seemed at that moment, as if all the elements in the atmosphere concentrated only on her.

Then Gururani began singing. The strains of her voice floated effortlessly — oblivious of the occasional protests of her throat at being taken through long uncharted territory.

Indu's feet moved and her face registered the different *mudras* of the *abhinaya*. Gururani delightfully kept *taal* by clapping her hands and on one occasion even got carried away to twirl shyly in perfect sync with Indu.

It was certainly not a perfect performance, interspersed as it was by much giggling and frequent stopping and starting, but it was one that its participants enjoyed more than any other. At last a huffing and puffing Gururani plonked herself on the diwan and somewhat sheepishly began to wipe the sweat from her brow with the end of her saree pallav.

Indu walked upto her. "You have shown me the way, Gururani. But now I can't stay here any longer," she said. And then Indu turned to make her way to Rahul's room to pack her bag.

A bewildered Gururani followed her there, "No don't go. What will I tell your Guruji?"

"Gururani you will tell him that he's not my Guru anymore. I found my true Guru... someone whom I look up to and who has done all that I don't know if I can or will ever be able to do," she answered.

Indu removed the ghungroos from her ankles and placed them beside Gururani's feet. She then knelt in front of Gururani and placed her forehead at Gururani's feet in reverence...

5

A Clean Slate

A Clean Slate

"It is easier to make the break now.... You're only six months into the marriage, so if it does break now the wound will heal quickly," the counsellor told her, his voice full of genuine concern.

"But maybe if I continue my attempts for just a few weeks more... maybe giving it some more time will..." Bhavna began.

"So that you feel you did your utmost and only then gave up on it?" asked Dr Jha.

This man was amazing, thought Bhavna. He was voicing her thoughts completely — right down to the exact words they were being framed in.

"Mrs Bhavna Mehta you have been coming to me for three months now. Despite my and, I'm sure, your entreaties too, Mr Mehta has never come here with you. He doesn't even want to admit that he... or your marriage are faced with a problem. Mrs Mehta I, as your counsellor, can now safely say that now my priorities have shifted from saving your marriage, to saving you. So far, you have been the only sane partner in this marriage, and now you need to get out of the marriage as fast as you can if you want to retain your sanity."

"I realise that doctor. But it's just that I would never have dreamt that one day my marriage would be a failure," said Bhavna.

Bhavna darted a look at Dr Jha and her eyes welled over.

"These are exactly the thoughts they all feel.... All those women who can see the writing on the wall that's proclaiming the end of their marriage but refuse to read it. You are not alone in what you're going through. Nor are you to blame for it in any way," he said, staring at her. At this moment Bhavna was convinced that Dr Jha was a hypnotist and not a counsellor.

"A man of Keval's class who comes home drunk almost everyday... passes out soon after and then wakes up his wife in the middle of the night to force himself upon her night after night — with no apologies either in the morning... with not a loving or appreciative word for her in all these six months? He's definitely not worth it.

"I don't think you need to be so harsh on yourself, Mrs Mehta. You deserve much better than that. I believe that, and you better start doing so too.... You have already tried your best. Now, you have to take the difficult decision to walk out," Dr Jha continued as he walked her to the door.

Bhavna reached home and started putting some of her clothes and her most precious ornaments into a small suitcase. Just a little less quickly and a lot more neatly than heroines in Hindi films who stuffed their belongings into their suitcases any which way, when they left home.

Despite Dr Jha's reassuring words Bhavna was afraid. She shut the suitcase and looked at the phone. Should she inform Papa she was coming back home or just land up there?

After a bit of thought Bhavna realised that it would be difficult to explain the situation to him properly over the phone. Better to leave, just plain and simple L-E-A-V-E she thought still staring at the phone, which suddenly came to life as if by her stare. She gingerly picked it up.

"Mrs Mehta," said Ranganathan softly. "There's been a freak

mishap at the site today about an hour ago," Ranganathan's voice had become even more soft, as if to soften the blow that was being struck by his words. "Sir was overseeing the work from the ground floor.... I was standing and taking notes right next to him... when a construction worker who was on the first floor accidentally dropped a brick. It fell on Sir's head. No... no... there was no bleeding... That's the funny part but I guess it didn't fall from too much of a height. The only thing is that Sir fainted on the spot so we brought him here. I'm calling you from the hospital but you don't worry Mrs Mehta he's almost conscious now.... You can come to City Centre Hospital. He's in Room No. 24."

Bhavna lifted the suitcase from the bed and put it by the side of the cupboard, so it would be as unobstrusive as possible. No, her plans to leave would not change but in the interest of social and humanitarian considerations, they would have to be somewhat postponed.

Half an hour later, Bhavna stood outside room 24 at the City Centre Hospital talking to Dr Bhargava who had been attending to Keval. "You will be the best judge in this matter Mrs Mehta. As doctors what really worries us a little in cases of head injuries is when there is no apparent outward injury as has happened with your husband.... Even a CAT scan sometimes doesn't give us the true picture about possible internal injuries or other damage to the brain. The brain is such a complex organ you know," he said.

"As of now, Mr Mehta seems fine and normal to us, but it is your close observation in the next few hours that will confirm that no memory loss or gap has occurred as a result of this impact. We'll come back to you in a while. But please remember that we're all there to help you Mrs Mehta and will do our best, come what may," said Dr Bhargava, extending his hand to wish her the best of luck.

Bhavna walked gingerly towards Keval's room. He looked up

at her and smiled, a smile more warm than she'd ever got from him in the last six months of their marriage. Keval extended his hand and clasped hers warmly. He winced in pain at this slight movement, and held the side of his head above his left ear. She noticed a bandage at the top of the ear lobe.

"Does your head hurt?" asked Bhavna with a touch of concern.

"No... but this bandage on the ear does.... The top of the ear tore just a little when the brick fell," he said turning his head to show her the damage. "The doctors realised it just a while ago."

"He remembers everything," thought Bhavna as she shrivelled a little. Then she reminded herself of the humanitarian cause and walked closer to him. She hesitated, then extended her hand and stroked his hair sympathetically. He shut his eyes as if in relief.

"I love you very much Bhavna," he muttered "You're the most beautiful and innocent wife in the world and I'm the luckiest man in the whole world to have you."

Bhavna stared at him with disbelief. This did not sound like her husband talking.

"Bhavna come and sit next to me," Keval pleaded as he patted the space on the bed beside his legs. She sat where he beckoned her to. "Bhavna, I'm slightly confused about this but... I think I haven't done much for you in all these months.... You deserve a lot of happiness from me. Bhavna... and I'll give it all to you. Do me a favour, Bhavna. When you go back home call Ranganathan and tell him to book us two tickets to Goa for this weekend. I'm definitely going to be out of here by then. We'll have the time of our lives there," he said his voice full of childish glee.

For six months she had hoped, waited and fantasised for something like this. He had never ever spoken or behaved with such affection. And yet, right at this moment hearing his loving words... his coarse behaviour, the past seemed but a mere memory to her.

"Is everything all right Mrs Mehta?" It was the concerned voice of Dr Bhargava, who had called her on the intercom.

"And what about your husband... what's your observation about him Mrs Mehta?"

"He's fine. He's unbelievably good," smiled Bhavna.

"Are you sure Mrs Mehta? Please don't come to any hasty conclusions. Take your time but be sure to check for any kind of memory lapses... for the earlier they are brought to our notice, the earlier we could decide on a course of action or medication that might help him come to normalcy. Maybe you could try and jog his memory a little to be completely sure," continued the doctor.

"No, there is no need to do anything. He is perfectly normal... I want to take him back home right away doctor. He doesn't need any medicines," said Bhavna firmly.

"As you like Mrs Mehta," said Dr Bhargava.

Bhavna no longer needed Dr Jha to give her the strength to do what she now needed to. She herself was strong enough to do what she had to do.

Bhavna was not going to unpack that suitcase now. It would certainly be useful for the trip to Goa.

6

Waxworks

Waxworks

They were seated on adjacent chairs at the beauty parlour. For want of much else to do while waiting for the bleaching cream on her face to dry, Bulbul looked at the woman's image in the mirror in front of her.

Her closely set and thin, arched eyebrows reminded her of the bunny hops that her four-year-old daughter practised in her handwriting book. The very thought made Bulbul smile. The white dust of talcum powder was clearly discernible on the woman's brown skin. She seemed so small, as she sat there on the large parlour chair. A gaunt shrivelled up scarecrow-like creature. Who would ever find such a woman appealing, thought Bulbul, even as she realised what a mean thought that was in the very next instant.

The woman moved forward to the edge of her seat as she peered into the mirror in front, checking the colour of the roots of her hair. She caught Bulbul looking at her image in the mirror and proceeded to give Bulbul's image in her mirror a wide smile in return. Then, all of a sudden as though jolted to reality, her face stiffened.

"Suzy!" she called out, in a shrill voice that had suddenly turned angry. "I'll teach you a lesson Suzy! How dare you treat me like this! I've been waiting here ten minutes and no one is attending to me. What's going on in here?" she shrieked, much to the surprise of Bulbul. It was at this point that Bulbul noticed that the woman's front teeth protruded and that there were also scores of wrinkles on her neck. Too much skin and little flesh, thought Bulbul, and for once she felt less despairing of her own plumpness.

Suzy entered the room from the ante-room with a puzzled look. She took one look at the woman and connected, that she was the one who had shouted out her name. She sighed with exasperation as she made her way to Bulbul.

Showing her back to the gaunt woman defiantly, Suzy started to touch the white cream bleach on Bulbul's face and found its foam come off easily. "You can wash it off now madam," she told Bulbul gently.

By now the woman had left her chair and was standing just behind Bulbul. "Suzy!" she shouted, "You have time for everyone else, but me." The next moment she toned her voice down, "Don't I pay for all my treatments and... and don't you remember the big tip I gave you the last time?" she continued with indignation.

Bulbul found it difficult to understand what was going on. Suzy never ever behaved like this with anyone. She could not help but stare at the stone-faced Suzy who was now putting away an assortment of combs and scissors into a holder, oblivious of the woman's remonstrations.

Bulbul made her way to the wash-basin near the entrance to the ante-room. She splashed water and gently rubbed off the bleach from her face. Before she could reach for a tissue on the adjoining rack, Suzy was already dabbing her face for her. Bulbul was really surprised that Suzy was so completely unaffected by the utterances of the gaunt woman as she proceeded to examine Bulbul's face for the effect of the bleach.

Bulbul was uncomfortable with the strange vibes in the room. Suzy held Bulbul's chin up. She arched her face, then turned it to the right and then the left, looking at it from various angles, satisfied at the soft golden glow that shone in the light. She declared with pleasure, "Your face is glowing madam."

Suzy beckoned to Bulbul, "Come on Madam, we'll go for the facial to the ante-room."

"Suzy, what about that client outside? What's the matter? Why aren't you attending to her?" asked Bulbul. She knew it was none of her business and yet, she could not hold her curiosity any longer.

"Oh, I am sure that one of the others will attend to her sooner or later if she keeps whining and complaining. You need stamina to deal with her, and today I just don't have that kind of energy," Suzy said matter-of-factly.

"Is she a difficult customer?" asked Bulbul.

"Not in the way that difficult customers are usually difficult. Difficult customers are exacting, they want perfection, which is tiring but understandable for us. This one is a weirdo."

Bulbul smiled to herself at Suzy confiding in her. She knew that she herself was a really easy customer. It came naturally to her, for she was an easy person. Despite knowing that she was paying for being attended to, Bulbul always felt there was something so utterly feudal about being in a beauty parlour that she couldn't bear to be more vain than the situation demanded. She guiltily enjoyed her monthly makeover here, but could never bring herself to demand more attention than was regularly given to her. And to give Suzy her due, she in any case always did a good job of her task of transformation.

"I don't understand," Bulbul said. "In what way is she weird?" she asked as she went to lie down on the bunk in the ante-room. The room was full of the smell of boiling wax that bubbled in a saucepan on the hot plate near the entrance of the ante-room. It was just like the aroma of caramelising sugar — an unusual smell but one that Bulbul loved, just the way some people inexplicably loved the aroma of petrol. She inhaled it deeply.

"You lie down and take your face massage, madam," said Suzy. "I will tell you why I'm behaving like that with her," she said.

Suzy started to work on Bulbul's face. She made gentle, circular movements with her finger tips on both her cheeks, working from behind Bulbul's head.

"Mrs Nair. Her name is Mrs Nair," said Suzy "She stays just down the road. She has been coming here for thirty-odd years and I have seen her from the time my mother used to attend to her and I used to merely watch her. Mummy told me that her husband had taken one look at her on their wedding night and had been devastated. They hadn't let him see her before that. You know how Hindus had these strict arranged marriages till about a generation ago.

"He simply couldn't bear to think that he would have to spend his whole life with her. So at the first available opportunity, he left to go to the Gulf, leaving her here in his flat down the road, pretending he'd call her once he had settled down in his job.

"Everyone knows that he has married again in the Gulf and even has his own family. He hasn't returned in all these years but the man can't bear to tell this woman the truth. Yet he continues to send her money for her upkeep every month.

"Though people have tried to hint to her about the truth, she doesn't believe them. She doesn't want to believe them. She feels that since he sends her money every month, he still cares for her and will surely return one day.

"She has a comfortable amount of money to spend and nowhere really to spend it. Over the years, she is getting mentally affected — Alzheimer's disease some people say — and I too agree that there's something really wrong with her. She comes to the parlour every two to three days, saying she wants to be in perfect shape for him when he returns.

"She sees imaginary unwanted hair on her arms just two days after we have waxed it and pesters us to repeat the entire procedure all over again. And she insists; just because she is willing and able to pay for it.

"In the last couple of years she's been coming to us to dye her hair even when there is just half a millimeter growth of white hair at the roots. She is simply paranoid about greying. For a long time now, she has lost her sense of time and imagines that her husband left for the Gulf only a couple of weeks ago," explained Suzy.

"It has been thirty years, thirty long years, but she still imagines that he will soon send for her. Madness, sheer madness," concluded Suzy shaking her head from side to side.

"Do you know madam that she keeps asking us why she is greying as she is only in her twenties? Once she even accused one of my girls of tampering with the hair dye and permanently damaging her hair. Imagine!"

Suzy's usually gentle movements on Bulbul's face were turning more vigorous in tandem with her animated monologue.

"I simply don't know how to deal with a woman like that. I can't drive her away and I cannot reason with her either. I feel sorry for her, and at the same time angry too. Angry with her and angry with her husband too. Angry also, with our own hypocrisy. Why doesn't someone dare to tell her the stark truth? Why can't she understand and accept it?" she continued.

"I wonder if it will ever happen but I hope at least for our sake, that it happens soon. I'm at my wit's end handling this woman and her crazy demands. But the only thing is, how are we to tell her? And how will she take it when she is told?" said Suzy despairingly as she began to wipe out the excess cream from Bulbul's face with a cotton swab.

"This is how she will take it," said a voice behind them. A shocked Bulbul opened her eyes. A horrified Suzy turned around. Mrs Nair stood behind, glaring at them.

She had heard everything that Suzy had been saying all this while, and now stood there holding the saucepan that had been boiling with wax.

"Here's to both you beautiful women!" she said, as she hurled the hot molten wax in their faces. And her banshee-like laughter merged with their screams of burning horror.

7

Insane and Able

Insane and Able

Anjana had all the time in the world now to reflect and philosophise. In fact she really had nothing better to do, for her beseeching, crying and bouts of hysterical insistence that she was actually normal, had left everyone at the asylum unmoved. If anything, it had made the doctors and attendants there even more convinced that she was indeed a mental patient. They all knew with experience that every lunatic genuinely believes that his is the sole voice of sanity in an otherwise loony world. In just a few days here, Anjana had realised the futility of her protestation and had therefore stopped remonstrating.

Forced to be a quiet observer, Anjana had also stumbled upon another ironic realisation — that true happiness was to be found only in the minds of the insane. The insane, who were the sole inhabitors of their own private universes, did not depend on other people for their happiness. Sane people who did, were more often than not unhappy. Going by the same logic, Anjana was completely unhappy, and therefore completely sane. She was more sure of this fact in the asylum than she had ever been in the world of the sane outside.

Anjana bit her lip at the thought of how much easier she had made Vishwa's task. That's what landed her here today by her constant and honest admissions of feelings of inadequacy and inferiority when she had been with him. She looked all around her, as if to belie the disbelief she felt even now, at having landed here.

Except for her, each one of the eleven inhabitants of the dorm were fast asleep. The pale moonlight streaming in shafts through the two windows, seemed to bounce around the room, reflected by the cream coloured night suits that each of the women wore.

Ever since Anjana had passed out of boarding school, she had never imagined that she would have to spend a night in a dormitory again. She had married soon after and this was hardly the sort of place one would associate with a woman who had a husband and a child.

Yet here she was, in the prison of the mind, where sleep had eluded her every single night in these last few weeks, just like it had faithfully today. By now she had even lost track of time — it simply stretched in a vast unsurmountable sea in front of her, marked only by the ripples of her constant incomprehension at how and why her world had fallen apart in this last one year.

It was just about a year ago that she had returned home from hospital with her newborn son Arush. She had hoped so much that Arush would be able to bring colour to their lives as a couple and that he would help them finally feel like a family.

Arush had made her feel so wanted. He was the first human being who made his preferences for her so loud and clear that she felt like the most desirable woman on earth.

In those early few weeks it had seemed that she was nothing except a mother, a feeling that she had smugly accepted until that fateful afternoon when she realised what her motherhood had really cost her.

Anjana had just started nursing three week old Arush. She could hear her sister Gudiya — who had come from Bangalore to be with her for a few weeks after her delivery — clearing the vessels in the kitchen after lunch. She herself was sinking into a delicious nap even as Arush continued to suckle at her breast as she lay sideways. She was vaguely aware that she must soon sit up and hold Arush upright to make him burp, but sleep completely overtook her. And it was only when she felt a sticky wet feeling on her chest that she awoke suddenly.

Arush had thrown up his feed and spluttered helplessly in his own vomit. A panic-stricken Anjana picked him up and ran, shouting for help towards the spare bedroom which Gudiya had been given.

She burst the door open and stood transfixed. A naked Vishwa was upon Gudiya, making love to her as she moaned with pleasure. Anjana screamed and ran back to her room. She put Arush on the bed and stared at him. He had recovered by himself and showed only tell-tale signs around his mouth of the mess he had made.

Anjana wiped him vigorously — almost as though she were wiping away from her mind the scene that she had just seen. But that was certainly not to be. For the more she tried, the more the import of what she had seen that afternoon sank into her.

Now it all made sense to her — Gudiya's preferences to manage Anjana's house rather than attend to her when she was in hospital, the indulgent glances that Vishwa gave his sister-in-law, her insistence on serving Vishwa his meals fresh and hot. It was not Gudiya's girlish enthusiasm for living up to responsibilities — it was the sign of Gudiya's discovery of passion with Vishwa. The lust of a polio-afflicted girl who had not been able to find a timely and legitimate outlet for her desires for want of a suitable groom.

It was a double betrayal, but after the initial shock Anjana came to terms with the fact that she might be able to forgive Gudiya her sin. She was so young after all, and more importantly she was her own kin. It was Vishwa who she found more difficult to forgive — firstly for being a man and therefore more in control of the situation, and secondly for the object of the deceit.

But forgiveness as an issue did not even arise, as Anjana was soon to learn. Having discovered a certain magic of passion together, and already having been damned for it, Vishwa and Gudiya together decided that they did not need Anjana's lifelong martyrdom. They needed instead to have her out of the way, in order to rework their future together — after all everything was fair in love and war. And so it was due to their efforts that Anjana was here at the asylum.

It was amazing how quickly Vishwa had been able to stage-manage Anjana's 'madness' to be medically certified. If she chose to remain silent on the cause of her prolonged postnatal depression, the doctors would concur with Vishwa that she was in chronic and therefore dangerous depression. And if she took the risk, as she did on two occasions, to reveal the double betrayal as the cause of her shattered feelings, she was marked out as a hallucinating schizophrenic. Either way Vishwa and Gudiya walked away with all the sympathy, for having to manage her poor son Arush, who now had to be kept away from a 'dangerous' mother. It was therefore decided by professional opinion that Anjana should best be kept confined in the interests of both mother and child.

Oh! how Anjana ached for Arush, whose birth had brought nothing but trauma in its wake for her. How she longed to hold him upright as she used to and feel the soft down of his head as he chewed her shoulder to indicate his hunger. How she longed for him to grab at her breast and drain her until she felt as dry and thirsty as an Indian summer.

Anjana opened the first two buttons of her night shirt and ran her hands over her breasts to re-live the sensations that she had just been thinking about. But her touch was like an insult to them and made her feel even more barren than before. Not only was it impossible to come anywhere near what the real thing had been — it also made her cringe and feel ashamed of herself. What if someone saw what she sat doing at this moment — they might be justified in concluding that she was really loony. A lunatic woman who had to satisfy her ache to be touched, by her own self.

Anjana recalled her last few days at home. In Gudiya's eyes, she had then at least rarely seen the guilt of helpless want. She also still had too many memories of Gudiya as the pathetic little sister that overshadowed the justifiable hatred she felt for her now. Anjana realised that she wanted no vengeance on her own flesh and blood, beyond denying her the one whom she wrongfully lusted for.

But Vishwa? A man who had fed like a vulture on one sister's faith and another's vulnerability? His words to the Doctor still singed in her ears. "Imagine the crazy insinuations she makes. She's certainly a mental case to talk about her own sister like that. She just doesn't know what she says and does," he had said as he had admitted her here.

Anjana wished for the nth time that he would die as horrifically as ready meat for the vulture — whose soul she knew he actually possessed. And he deserved no mercy, for he was certainly not her own flesh and blood. If only she would get one chance to wreak vengeance on him she would do so. What stopped her was not a fear of punishment — it was only a lack of opportunity. She was not afraid of punishment, for now she had nothing more left to lose anyway. Nothing much, except missing the sights of her baby, Arush, growing up.

Would Arush ever know the truth about her? Anjana certainly hoped so. She did not know how, but someday, somehow, she did want to be able to tell him everything herself. It was the one hope that refused to die in her pining breast. She could not afford to die, if only for Arush and his future.

Anjana pulled the sheet upto her neck and shut her eyes. But shutting off the world did not drive away the quiet desperation that was now her constant companion. She soon opened her eyes, got up from the bed and walked to the small window to the left of her bed. She felt the breeze caress her face and teasingly ruffle her coarse hair as though it was attempting to break the morbid stillness of her life. The pages of the calendar fluttered with a crackle and then settled again. Anjana looked at the picture of Gandhiji — his toothless, beatific grin looking in her direction, and her eyes fell on the words printed at the bottom of the picture, "Find purpose and the means will follow." Easier said than done thought Anjana, but true nevertheless. She would have to find a focus, if she was to last out until Arush came of age — and she would have to find it fast.

Anjana searched hard and that was why she found it soon enough. Found it in fact the very next morning in the form of Snehlata Deshpande's new scheme for the women inmates at the asylum.

Snehlata was a radical-thinking woman who had been appointed the warden of the asylum only two months ago. She had declared to all those associated with the place that she believed in finding positive solutions to the most pressing practical problems they were having there. Now she had found one to solve the perennial problem that the asylum faced in attracting staffers to do the poorly paid labour-intensive jobs in running the place. If the inmates could be guided to do the jobs themselves, it would not only keep them fruitfully occupied but would also help them earn a salary.

Snehlata gathered all the thirty-five inmates of the home in the courtyard the next morning and explained her plan. She announced that she would guide and review their work and also make sure that the money they earned was put aside in their accounts — which they could either give their dependents, or save up for themselves to use when they left the asylum to face the world outside.

Most of them gathered there felt that Snehlata's rehabilitation plan was just a new rule they would have to follow there. It was only Anjana who walked upto her, her eyes full of gratitude and appreciation for the focus that this plan had just given her. Snehlata, who was taken aback by Anjana's intelligent response, stared hard at Anjana. Something unspoken passed between the two of them that moment and a bond was formed instantly.

Snehlata knew that Anjana was not like everyone else. And in the forthcoming weeks Snehlata was vindicated in what she had felt at that moment — without even once discussing it openly with her. Anjana came to be entrusted by Snehlata with the most trustworthy job at the asylum — that of running the kitchen. In no time at all, she took it over completely. From morning until dusk, Anjana rushed about — chopping, cooking, cleaning and directing the five women who had been assigned to assist her. It was something that she was used to doing, as she had run her home with Vishwa with remarkable organisation and competence — until that dark day when she had discovered his true colours.

In a few weeks time Anjana came to symbolise the success of Snehlata's rehabilitation scheme. She became a virtual exhibit for both the inspection staff who occasionally visited the asylum, as well as for the few relatives of the inmates who sometimes called on them. She was an embodiment of hope and living proof of the fact that a mental patient could lead a fruitful and dignified life and maybe even recover.

And then, one day, Vishwa came visiting. Snehlata led him proudly into the kitchen to watch Anjana who sat on the floor finely shredding her way through half-a-dozen cabbages with utter concentration, totally oblivious of their presence. Vishwa watched silently for a few moments.

Then Snehlata prodded him to stop hesitating and they both walked towards her. Anjana looked up at Vishwa's forlorn face. A wave of anger lashed at her. She knew that he had only come to confirm the state of her condition for his future plans. She listened quietly as he pretended to brighten up when Snehlata praised Anjana.

Snehlata told him that at the rate at which Anjana was making a positive impression, she might soon be completely normal and therefore be allowed to go home. She added that they would all miss her at the asylum, but that Anjana surely deserved better.

Vishwa looked confused as Snehlata urged him to go closer to Anjana and talk to her. Snehlata turned to walk away a few yards — to facilitate the hesitant and tender husband and wife intimacy that she thought might follow. Vishwa had no option but to comply and went closer to Anjana. Snehlata smiled contentedly as she neared the exit door. But she soon stopped in her tracks — at the sound of a blood-curdling scream.

She turned around, horrified to see Anjana repeatedly stabbing a screaming Vishwa with her kitchen knife and watched aghast as he slumped to the ground in a pool of blood upon the pile of shredded cabbage.

"This is the man who said I was mad, when I wasn't. And he's paying for it now. This proves that I'm mad doesn't it?" she screamed as she drove the knife again and again into a Vishwa who lay there with a stunned look on his face, feeling life slowly draining out of him.

Snehlata ran towards Anjana and pulled her away from Vishwa as Anjana continued ranting. "It is your gift of madness Vishwa, which has today enabled me to wreak vengeance on you, without any fear of punishment," she screamed, as she threw the blood-soaked knife to a corner.

"I'm a certified mental case. How can I be punished for this... in my madness I don't even know what I say or do. Didn't you yourself say that about me Vishwa? Answer me, didn't you?" she hollered.

But Vishwa did not answer.

8

Screaming Silence

Screaming Silence

The meeting was about to begin when Mrs Sharma, late and out of breath, burst into the roomful of people in Mr Mehta's house.

"I'm sorry — very sorry," she declared to everyone and yet no one in particular, as her eyes darted from one end of the room to another.

Mrs Mehta and Mrs Patil squeezed up closer to create some place for Mrs Sharma to sit between them on the settee.

Mrs Mehta smiled at her. "Overslept the afternoon nap did you?" she asked as she looked at her watch. "I guess five o'clock is a bit early in the evening. But Mehta*sahab* insisted you should all be here by this time — so perhaps you could hear for yourself the goings-on in the neighbouring house. You just cannot imagine how disturbing and upsetting it is for us," she explained.

"Of course we can imagine," said Mr Patil forcefully, from the men's end of the room.

"We are just below that horrible man and we too can hear all his abuses, beatings and thumpings every evening, day after day. It's worse if we come out into the balcony — I tell you i haven't heard such a choice of abuses even in the filthiest book I've ever read," he continued.

"Deva, Deva, Mahadeva. What is the world coming to," said Mr Narayan touching his ears alternatively with the fingertips of both his hands as if to wipe out the sounds that had assailed them in the last few days.

"Such a nice, peaceful atmosphere we had in this building before this rascal came onto the scene," said Mr Das. "It's all that Deshpande's fault. He should have properly checked that swine Adhikari out, before renting the flat to him."

"It's not his fault Mr Das. It's impossible to completely check out a person's character before you let out your place. How could Deshpande ever have imagined that this Mr Adhikari would turn out to be such a scoundrel? He seemed a normal man even to me when I visited him on the first day that he arrived next door. I went to meet him and offered him any help he might need, just as any good neighbour should do," said Mr Mehta.

"Yes, but you did mention to me that he didn't even call you inside the house that evening," piped in Mrs Mehta.

"Yes that's true. But I didn't make much of it at that time. He came to the door still dripping from his bath, wrapped only in a towel. I didn't expect him to call me inside in that state. He thanked me for my offer and said that he'd definitely get back to me soon. He seemed like a normal, a regular sort of chap. But in these last fifteen days that he's been here he hasn't paid a visit to anyone's house, I suppose?" Mr Mehta queried as he looked around. Everyone nodded their head to and fro, looking left and right to affirm the truth of Mr Mehta's statement.

"It would have been all right if he wasn't the mixing type — we don't mind that, do we?" said Mr Das "But the point is, we all live in a civilised society. How can we just hear him abuse and beat someone evening after evening and just pretend that we haven't heard anything?"

"Someone? What do you mean by someone? It's probably a woman — his wife —who else could it be? I'm absolutely sure that it's his wife whom he beats. Who else but a wife would tolerate such nonsense from a man?" asked Mrs Patil indignantly, as all the other women in the room nodded approvingly at her statement and the men listened stoically.

"That poor dear. She's probably closetted in her room all day. I've not seen her even once answering the door, or going shopping — you know, all the normal things women do."

"It's almost as if she doesn't exist," said Mrs Mehta.

"Who would want an existence like that anyway? Better to die than have to exist that way," said Mrs Patil, indignantly.

"I think it's time we women went to the help of our sister suffering in silent pain. It's women alone who have to take the lead in helping out one of their own," said Mrs Patil, almost rising to her feet, ready for action that very moment.

"Yes yes, we will not allow her to suffer even one day more. But we have to wait for the opportune moment if we are to catch him red-handed. I know people like that, they're aces at covering up their dirty deeds. So let's wait a bit and then pounce on him while he's at the poor soul today," said Mrs Sharma. "We'll go at his door and ring the bell continuously to scare the daylights out of him. No more of this nonsense, not for another day!" she continued righteously.

"Wait!" Mrs Mehta exclaimed. "I just realised that we have an even better way in which to swoop down on him. You remember old Mr Percy who used to stay here before Adhikari? He had given us a spare set of keys to his flat for safe keeping. Percy has forgotten to take them back from me. I still have the key to the main door with me. I don't think the rascal has changed the lock — so we can all probably enter the flat without even ringing the bell. That way he'll have no chance at all to cover up his tracks," said Mrs Mehta excitedly.

Mrs Mehta excused herself and went into her bedroom to rummage in the cupboard drawers for the all-important key. Soon she entered the hall triumphantly and noticed that the men and women were talking animatedly in several groups.

"Shh-Shh. I think if we all remain silent we can actually hear the thumping start. Everyday it starts around half past five. Its like a ritual for the beast. Hear, hear it carefully now," Mrs Mehta implored with a finger on her lips. And right enough in the hushed silence of the room, the by now unmistakable sounds began to build up.

"Thump- thump..... You bloody bitch. You swine...... here take this ....thump thump... what do you take me for .... I'm a bloody man ...... not a eunuch ....Take this ......and this ....thump ......smack ......thump .... I'll teach you a thing or two about dealing with me....," Adhikari ranted.

Mrs Sharma sprang to her feet. "That's it. We can't wait anymore. Let's go in right now or the poor soul will simply die...," she implored, as everyone rose to their feet.

"Wait, ladies wait. You all come right behind us. After all we do not want you women to be in harm's way. This man Adhikari, you never know what he might do in his anger," said Mr Mehta responsibly, as all the men gallantly followed him and the women took up the rear. Mr Mehta took the rather rusty key from his wife's hand and commanded her to fall back with the women. Touched at her husband's concern for her Mrs Mehta smilingly complied.

Mehta, Das, Patil and Narayan led the group as Mrs Mehta, Mrs Patil and Mrs Sharma walked behind them. They softly opened the main door of Mr Mehta's flat and soon stood right outside Mr Adhikari's door. Mr Mehta signalled to everyone to remove their footwear to eliminate any kind of noise, while they walked through the passage of Mr

Adhikari's house. They were all sure that these terrible sounds probably emanated from the inner bedroom.

Mr Mehta turned the key in Mr Adhikari's door. Thanks to its well oiled hinges it opened stealthily and noiselessly.

The sounds were loud and clear now and the women covered their ears, singed by their vitriolic content.

"You tart — you whore — you want me to respect you — you — bloody bitch. You think I don't know your true colours. Just because you sleep around with a rich guy you think you've become a decent woman and you can order me around? As for him, he's a parasite of the first order. He's had hundreds before you and will probably have hundreds after you in this very suite — you dare to throw your weight around with me? Who do you think you are? — Now I'm not going to take any more of your nonsense. Thump — smack, — here take this — that'll teach you to behave yourself," he went on.

The women looked somewhat quizzically at each other — his words did not make much sense. Besides, it sounded more like a monologue from up so close. Surely the woman he was beating would at least moan or groan in pain. "Has she become immune to the beatings by now? Was she already dead?" thought a stumped Mrs Mehta to herself as she followed the line inching forward. It was such a chilling thought. The men, by now very close to the door of the bedroom that was half shut, finally prepared themselves. Mr Mehta gave the door a push and took the lead in making their collective presence felt to Mr Adhikari.

"Stop, you bastard. Stop at once. Stop!" he said as the others joined in, in varied tones and with differed timings. Mr Adhikari was speechless upon spotting the crowd. He stood there gaping at first, and then made a hurried attempt to cover his naked upper body by crossing his chest with his fists on which were a pair of boxing gloves. Rivulets of sweat from his body had made his boxing shorts completely wet. The men's eyes now took in the punching bags above Adhikari's head that were still swinging with the effect of his attacks.

"Boxing — is that all you're upto every evening?" asked Mr Mehta, the feeling of loss so distinct in his voice.

"Yes, what did you think? But before I answer you, tell me is this how respectable neighbours make an entry into another man's home in this building?" asked Mr Adhikari as he removed his boxing gloves and wrapped a king-size Turkish towel around his torso, like a shawl.

There was only stunned silence that answered him.

"Will someone please explain what's going on?" asked Mr Adhikari as he led everyone through the passage into the hall.

As the group stood awkwardly around, he signalled to them to sit down on the sofas. "Don't tell me you need my permission to sit down when you didn't need it to enter my house," he remarked caustically.

"We're sorry, terribly sorry Mr Adhikari.. we hadn't the foggiest idea that you were only boxing," said Mr Mehta.

"We thought you were beating some poor soul — perhaps your wife — black and blue every single evening. We did it out of a sense of concern for her.... I mean who we thought was her," stuttered Mrs Mehta.

Mr Das hesitantly pitched in. "Sir, you cannot entirely put the blame on us. You must admit that your abuses — your ..... colourful language as you .....er ..... box ...... would make anyone suspicious. We didn't want to be heartless to the fate of someone who we thought was a poor, bruised soul staying next door to us. Of course it's a relief to know that nothing of the sort was going on here. We're really sorry Mr Adhikari....."

Mr Adhikari's disconcerted expression had somewhat softened by now. He sat down cross-legged on the floor, probably not wanting to soil the sofas with his still sweaty bottom.

"I will not leave your mystery half-solved. Now that you are here, I'd like to explain everything completely," he said.

"I'm not fond of beating anyone — that you have already ascertained. I hate abusing too. But it's part of my therapy," he said.

"Therapy?" asked everyone in complete unison.

"You see. I work as the lobby manager in a five-star hotel. All day long I've got to keep a straight, plastic smile across my face. I've got to mutter yes sir, no sir, yes madam, you're right madam, certainly sir, in a minute madam .... it's so sickening this 'customer is always right' nonsense. I can never be myself, never answer back, no matter how wrong or stupid the person I'm dealing with is. It's unfair and unjust, and after a few months at the job, I realised that I wouldn't be able to cope."

"Then I tried psychotherapy. I gave myself a last chance to see if I could cope with my job that way."

"My psychotherapist suggested a therapy for this, a kind of catharsis, which involves the release of pent-up emotions. He suggested that since I couldn't afford to open up my feelings at work, I should release my frustrations by doing all that I could possibly not do at work — in the privacy of my bedroom. Perhaps I overdid the abuses but let me tell you that the therapy has really worked for me! Today, for example, I was punching the bags pretending to beat and abuse this arrogant mistress of a filthy rich old man — who ordered me around all day. D'you think its easy for me to go back for her kicks tomorrow if I don't punch these bags today? This therapy really works... it does! Well since it has worked so well for me, and now that you all also know what it's all about, I'd like your permission to keep at it every evening! Is it fine by you all?" he asked.

"Yes, yes by all means it's fine. We'll all find some way of coping with the sounds — after all it's all for a good cause isn't it?" said Mr Das with a chuckle. A couple of handshakes and *namastes* later the troop left and Mr Adhikari went back to punching his bags.

And the residents of the building did find a perfect way of coping with these sounds indeed, from that very evening. Just a few minutes later each one of them was heady with the therapeutic effects of his or her pounding, punching and abusing, within the safe confines of their bedrooms.

9

Face to Face

Face to Face

FOR REFERENCE ONLY, stated the familiar purple ink stamp on the first page of the library book that Aparna had found with such difficulty at the end of that afternoon. Faded but legible enough to put an end to her hopes of leaving the library early that afternoon with the book and spending the extra time with Amod. Now there was absolutely no chance of her being able to take the book home to make notes for Friday's tutorial. Frankly, it was lucky enough that she had found this book to study all to herself in this foreign library. The two copies of *Slavic Wars* in the college library had constantly been in circulation and therefore had been difficult to lay her hands on, these past two weeks.

Aparna carried the book and walked to sit in the corner of the second table, ready with her foolscap sheets and ball-point pen. She opened the chapter on Wars of the Roses, langorously slicing the pages that had stuck together through disuse. It made a delicious crackling sound. The book had obviously rarely ever been opened! She then mentally calculated that she would definitely be able to finish making notes in the next two to three hours, for her reference chapter was only about forty pages long.

It was then that Aparna's eyes first met the 'muffler' woman's. She came to sit diagonally opposite Aparna soon after Aparna had settled into her chair. A distinguished fifty year old, she had a cropped, no-nonsense haircut on her salt and pepper hair. More salt than pepper actually.

That day she had worn a saree, but Aparna was to see her later in many attires — and so many avatars. Sometimes in salwar-kurtas, sometimes in trousers and once even in a long Tibetan Baku dress. She was certainly well preserved — the sort of woman who could easily look ten to fifteen years younger if she dyed her hair. But whatever it was that she chose to wear, the muffler was always there — covering her neck as protectively as though it were hiding a woman's secret.

The muffler-woman had sat opposite Aparna reading a hard-cover, that looked so much like the reference book that Aparna was working from. It was strange, Aparna had thought at that time — these kind of reference books were hardly leisure reading. Most people who scanned them, tended to make jottings. Maybe she was a lecturer or a research professor. Well! she certainly must be top notch for she did not seem to need to make any notes and was content with merely casually scanning the pages. But actually in hindsight her expression that afternoon, was more of disinterest than supreme confidence.

That day Aparna had gone on to make long copious notes. About half an hour after she had started she had lifted her tired eyes from the page that she had been writing on. The muffler-woman she noticed, was staring at her. But the moment Aparna's eyes met hers, she immediately looked away. Aparna also noticed that the woman still seemed to be at the halfway mark of the volume; where she had been an hour ago. A highly distracted professor she was, Aparna had then thought!

The woman closed her book with a bored look and coughed softly. It was surprising how one sniffle or cough in the silence of the library seems to be like a clarion call for others to follow suit. For a few minutes after that, there was a virtual wave of such pent-up releases from the people present and, then a gradual petering out. And right enough, soon the familiar silence descended once again. Aparna saw the woman exit soon after.

The second time had been at the local supermarket. Aparna saw her there again, walking through the aisle, browsing through the goods on the shelves. The muffler-woman would pick up the occasional jar or packet, examine it distractedly and then put it right back in its original place. Aparna meanwhile was busy, dutifully tick-marking the list of items that her mother had jotted down, as she put them one by one in the trolley. Each time she looked up across the shelf, she would catch the muffler-woman looking at her. It seemed like such an eerie coincidence seeing her this often, she thought — it was almost as if the woman had been following her every move.

But then, as Aparna rationalised, the woman could be justified in feeling exactly the same way about her. Aparna tried not to think about it anymore as she noticed that the woman nervous and somewhat distractedly, again checked out the same packets of soup and noodles that she had just a few seconds earlier.

Aparna caught her staring at her once again. She fought a sinking feeling at the pit of her stomach and gave the muffler — woman a broad smile. She was determined to humour her for now. After all, coincidences do leave one with an unnerving feeling. And they were possibly nothing more than mere coincidences.

She was sure that the woman would smile right back at her. And smile she did — a frightened and forced smile, like a child who is forced to smile in the name of bravery just after the pain of an injection.

The muffler-woman proceeded to shuffle away — leaving a distinct distaste in Aparna's mouth. For the first time in their coincidental interactions, a shiver went down Aparna's spine. She had to acknowledge an uncomfortable feeling that perhaps she was indeed being followed, and the admission, then realisation, that perhaps these encounters may not be coincidental, was now too real and palpable.

Over the next few days such encounters were repeated ever so often. At Bandra railway station, at Jogger's Park where she jogged with Amod, at the Santacruz market where she shopped, at Fashion Street, even at Eros when she went to see a film with Amod, the muffler-woman always seemed to be watching her, yet she never seemed interested in befriending her.

Who was she? Why was she following Aparna? Could she be a private detective? Aparna did briefly consider it, but she ruled it out soon enough as the woman was getting caught all the time. Surely that was one of the elementary things that detectives were taught to avoid. In any event, who in the world could possibly want to put a detective on her and why?

Could it be Amod? No, he certainly didn't seem the kind. Besides, he had no reason at all to be suspicious of her. So did no one else for that matter. But if she were not a detective, who was she after all? After about a dozen such silent encounters, the mystery was now getting a little too perplexing for Aparna.

Suspense of this kind was exciting so long as it happened in the pages of a book, where all the answers lay a few pages away. And if, like Amod, one was too impatient to wait even for that, one could always skip pages to crack the mystery in advance. But this was the real thing, and it was leading Aparna's mind in the most bizarre directions. At this rate she was in danger of completely losing her peace of mind if she did not get to the bottom of the mystery soon.

Was the muffler-woman a serial killer in search of prey? Was she a lesbian? Or maybe someone secretly connected with the family? A secret mistress of her father? Now that Aparna thought about it, there had been more than the normal mom-sobbing-behind-shut-bedroom-door and dinner-getting-cold-on-the-table scenes these last few weeks at home.

But then in the end, Mom and Dad did seem to get over whatever problems they had had. Just like it had always been. And somehow Aparna was sure that Mom and Dad's problems were more related to their differing opinions on how to deal with close relatives, or due to Dad's occasional drinking excesses. Surely the muffler-woman could not in any way be related to such family problems. In spite of this, Aparna thought it wise not to share her anxiety about the woman with anyone in the family just yet.

But she also knew that she had to share it with someone else for she was feeling too suffocated to deal with it on her own. That someone could only be Amod, and perhaps this would be a nice way of testing really how much he cared for her, thought Aparna.

Amod laughed his guts out when she first mentioned the muffler-woman. Aparna was offended and she got up in a huff from her chair in the college canteen. But as she was about to walk away, he caught her hand and realised that it was so very cold. At that moment Amod's expression changed and he became serious. He made her sit down and pour out all her worries to him. "Don't worry," he reassured her, "we will crack the mystery very soon."

Amod put his arms protectively around Aparna's shoulders. "Come on," he said "I'll drop you to the station. You're in time for the 4:25 local and if you are any later you will get caught in the office rush going homewards. Let's hurry it's 4:00 o'clock already," he said.

They walked silently, hand-in-hand, each preoccupied with their own thoughts, making their way to the northern end of platform number one. The huge clock in the concourse showed 4:07 pm and the indicator for platform 1 showed that the train would depart at 4:25 pm. Suddenly, Aparna noticed the indicator for platform 3 reading '4:09 Andheri fast'. Catching that would be a good idea, she thought.

Aparna told Amod that she had decided to cross the tracks and go across to platform 3, so she could catch the faster train. She had done this many times earlier too, so she bid Amod a quick good-bye and he watched her scurry away with some concern.

Aparna hurried down the slope of platform 1 to go onto platform 2. Suddenly there was a rude push and she was thrown with a hard thud to her right. She was about to protest indignantly when right at that moment, she saw a train pass her by on the track she had intended to cross.

In a flash it dawned upon her as she reeled to recovery — someone had just saved her life!

A crowd had gathered by now. Amod was by her side in seconds and helped her to her feet. Aparna was about to turn to walk back onto the platform, when she saw the face of the muffler-woman lying on the ground. There she was staring at her like always, but this time with still eyes. Her torso had just been crushed by the train that had passed by. It was her familiar chilling stare all right, now frozen forever.

It was the muffler-woman who had saved her life! She had tripped onto the track while shoving Aparna aside — the rude push that had saved Aparna's life had come from her! Aparna stared at her with a blend of fascination, gratitude and horror as she lay dead.

Amod tried to pull Aparna away but she clutched his hand firmly and whispered hoarsely into his ear. "It's her, it's the muffler-woman... the one I was telling you about." A stunned Amod then inched towards the body. He noticed faint, bruise marks on either side of her neck. At close sight, she looked sad and vulnerable, with a hunted-animal expression on her face. In her lifeless hand the muffler-woman still clutched an envelope that now fluttered in the breeze, held precariously in a grip between her thumb and fore finger. Amod bent down, picked up the envelope and led Aparna away.

Amod and Aparna sat down on the bench on the platform. He opened the envelope and began to read softly.

My dear Aparna,

In these last few weeks I have given you many worrisome moments indeed, with my horribly strange behaviour. I write this letter to you now, so that these worries can finally be put to an end. Indeed, worry is the last reaction I should evoke in you. In fact, I pray that the Almighty puts all your burdens on my shoulders to bear, and that he should make me of some use to your life.

You wonder why a stranger should feel such love for you? You are not a stranger to me. You are — or to make the matter easier for you to understand — you were my daughter.

My daughter, my only child, died a slow and painful death due to cancer twenty years ago in my arms when she was only four. I tried everything that a mother in my place tries, to get over her loss. But the truth is that I could not ever get over it. And the years went slowly by, somehow. Last year my husband left me too, and I was left all alone in this world. I tried Reiki, meditation and a whole lot of other new age therapies to be able to cope with my loss.

I even tried to commit suicide. I tried to hang myself with a saree but couldn't get it right and was soon saved by a neighbour. It is the marks of that attempt that I hide with the muffler that I always wear around my neck.

Then last summer I met Vespi. Vespi communicates with those in the other world. And he helps tormented souls like mine to know that their loved ones are indeed there, that they are still alive, though in another body. He even tells us where and how they live.

Vespi promised to let me know where, and in which form, my daughter had been reborn. And it was he who told me that you were her, reborn in another home sixteen years ago!

Vespi warned me that I must not disturb you in your present life and that the knowledge of your past birth must be kept a secret only between the two of us.

I tried very hard to do that. I tried to leave you alone. But try as I might I could not resist wanting to watch you, my beautiful angel. For that was all the joy that I had left in my empty life. Yet, whenever your eyes would catch my glance I would wince. I was afraid that if you approached me at a weak moment, I would break my promise to Vespi and tell you what you were to me. And that would destroy your peace of mind. I loved you too much to want that to happen just because of me.

I write this letter only to end the torment that my mysterious behaviour has caused you. I am sad that I have had to break my promise to Vespi and also to disturb you with my truth, so the best way to atone for my wrong doing is to promise you that I will never see you again. It will kill me to do that but I promise that I shall stick to my word.

I will finally learn to be alone. Thank you, my daughter, for you have made me whole again, and with your beautiful memories I will be able to live alone. Live alone and die alone.

Your loving Mother.

10

Two Gold Guineas

Two Gold Guineas

PART 1

The critical 48 hours were almost up. Biji would surely pull through. As in the past she had once again proved to be a survivor, thought Achala as she looked at Biji's frail body slumped against the pillow on the impersonal hospital bed. Biji's dark lips looked so parched, for she had been breathing with her mouth slightly ajar. The black pepper corn-sized mole at the edge of her lip now shone even more prominently and centimetre long twin white hairs sprouted from its peak.

Achala touched the moistened cotton swab to her lips and Biji opened her eyes for a moment. Rolling her pupils as though she was peeping into her own eyelids, she looked like one possessed, before she shut them again.

Biji was fair, slim and short. Ever since Achala could remember, she had been dressed in a white salwar kameez that was always clean but never bright. At this moment too, everything about her was the same as it had always been. Her dull white salwar-kameez, her silver-turning-to-yellow hair neatly plaited. Only the familiar aroma of 'desi ghee' that enveloped her at home, had been punctured by the antiseptic and iodine smell so typical of a hospital. And the white chunni she covered her head with and then wrapped like a scarf around her neck had now slipped under her back as she lay supine on the bed.

Suddenly Achala noticed the two gold guineas that Biji always kept guarded in the knot of her chunni. To outsiders they appeared like the petty coins that old women often kept here, either to give beggars or offer to deities at temples.

It was just as well, thought Achala, for if they knew the value of those two gold guineas, many would not hesitate to conclude that the old woman's life was infinitely less worthy than the worth of the guineas. But though she always agreed that times were bad, Biji refused to see reason whenever Achala suggested that she remove the guineas and keep them somewhere safer.

Every morning when Biji prepared to go for her bath, she would undo the knot of the chunni she had been wearing, remove the guineas and then knot them into the edge of the fresh chunni which she was to wear soon after her bath.

The guineas were all that Bauji had been able to give her. He had told her that they were his only family heirlooms and were to be passed on to the first two members who joined the family tree by marriage – whether they were sons or daughters-in-law.

Biji often recounted how Bauji had himself knotted the guineas into her chunni as they prepared to leave their home in Lahore during the partition riots of 1947. Biji had then been pregnant, almost full-term, with Achala. A bewildered Bauji had held their four-year-old son Achal Kumar's hand in one hand, and supported Biji with another, as they tried to wend their way through the crowds approaching Lahore station to get onto the train going to Delhi. In the melee Achal Kumar, who had somehow loosened the grip of Bauji's hand, had got lost. A stunned Bauji had had to make the critical choice of clambering on the train to join his remaining family or stay behind to search for his son... And when he clearly couldn't decide, the crowd made the decision for him and he got swept along. Everyone around convinced him that the child had probably already been crushed under the feet of the waves of humanity that

surged towards the train. So now it was quick and prudently decided that it was better at least to escape with his wife and unborn child.

Achala had been born in a refugee camp — named in memory of, or as compensation for the lost Achal Kumar. In a short passage of time, Bauji virtually willed himself to death unable to live with the feeling of responsibility for Achal Kumar's loss. A stoic Biji plodded on, living as is wont with women, for the sake of their children. Biji brought up Achala alone, taking as much care of her as she did of the two gold guineas knotted in her chunni. Biji, Achala and the guineas— there were the same three of them in 1947 as there were today in this hospital room, thought Achala, glancing at the knotted guineas. Biji, Achala, and the guineas. Fifty years later as fifty years earlier. Amala it seemed, had come and gone from their lives like a teasing, fragrant breeze that they would both do anything to woo back into their arid existence.

Achala checked the drip of the intravenous tube that fed Biji's arm as the clock struck 12.00. She sat on the stiff wooden chair next to Biji's bed and opened her diary to its first page. It was time she kept the promise that she had made to herself. It was a momentous moment to begin her diary — the striking clock, had just heralded the completion of 50 years of her existence. If nothing, she must write to commemorate that there was yet nothing to commemorate. She began to write :

PART 2

It is a moment to celebrate but I have no one to celebrate it with, except frail, unconscious Biji with the two gold guineas knotted in her chunni and perhaps no one who will claim those guineas.

Jatin should logically have been the first claimant. Jatin — my lawfully wedded husband who left me nearly 20 years ago, consumed by an inexplicable spiritual wanderlust when our daughter, whom he had named Amala was just a few months old. Amala, he explained, meant the pure one. For once he had done right — in naming her, that is.

Jatin had, in the true tradition of the Buddha, set out to discover the meaning of life. He had left me without any warning, just disappeared one morning. For he had probably believed that if he didn't do it that way, he wouldn't ever be able to shake off the desires and bonds that tied him to this world of Maya. I had sensed that even on the few occasions that he had been romantic with me, he seemed to hate, even while loving me for being the object of his desire. His eyes never met mine when he made love and the act itself was more akin to the desperation of a man easing himself. And so after it was over, he always looked a mixture of relief and shame and half expected me to look guilty for having tempted him. I knew that for him I was completely symbolic of Manu's woman-is-a-necessary-curse-for- mankind philosophy.

To be really frank, I was actually relieved when he finally left — at least he had clearly made a decision. Never mind if I had to fend for myself, my daughter and my mother. At least he'd given me this lovely, beautiful child and caring for her became the sole focus of both Biji's and my life from then onwards.

It did not particularly bother me what the world thought of my marital status, or whether I qualified as widow or divorcee. At that time I didn't miss physical and emotional intimacy either — for I had never known it until Ravi came into my life. Till then, I was comfortable playing daughter, mother, and man of my home — for after Jatin left I had also to start earning a living to support Biji and Amala.

It was while playing this man's role that I met the man who would make me feel woman again — in fact more woman than I had ever felt in my life before. I joined Ravi's office as a secretarial assistant and ended up as what the world - if it had known about us - would call, his mistress.

Ravi was my boss at the office. Away from there, he was my pillar of support. He had always been there for me when I needed him. He was there when Amala needed to be admitted to a good school, when Biji had to undergo an emergency bypass surgery and on several other occasions. He enjoyed caring for me and often confessed, that it was only when he was with me that he in turn felt like a real man. Frankly I could never understand what he saw in me, for his wife Ketaki was stunning to look at. She was also a competent businesswoman — and would have been an asset to any modern man.

When I mentioned this to Ravi he had said that the difference between Ketaki and me was like the difference between synthetic and natural fabric. (After all he was the son-in-law of the founder of the famous Alliance Textile Mills!) Synthetic fibre always falls well but feels dead. The natural fabric — alive to the ravages of time and treatment often does not look as good but it breathes and is therefore confirmedly alive.

"You are my earth," Ravi would often say after we became lovers. I remember how much he hated it when I once dyed my greying hair. "Never do that again. You remind me of

Ketaki," he had said in a distinctly wounded voice.

Strange are the ways of life. Here was a man who wanted to give and care but whose wife did not want it. In fact, her complaint was that he was just not dynamic enough. For she, on her part was already a minor celebrity and was always working towards a higher profile for the textile company that she had inherited from her father.

Ravi and Ketaki had a modern marriage, an arrangement where each was left free to do their own thing, bound only by the slender thread of common concern for their son Vikram. The only problem was that deep in his heart Ravi did not believe in the concept of a modern marriage, while Ketaki happily seemed to have made the most of the arrangement.

It was for this reason (though I hate to think of myself as Ravi's mistress) that I probably appealed to Ravi. I was actually so much like a wife. And the fact that I didn't expect much from Ravi made him want to give and care all that much more. And so he cared and I bloomed in our memorable years of togetherness.

Yes I did so often question myself. I questioned our love. I felt guilty about the immorality of what I was doing, but Ravi always reassured me. He explained, that except in the eyes of the world, he really had no marriage going with Ketaki.. So I was no 'other woman'. I was the only real woman for him.

Both of us were committed to our roles as providers to our families, and as parents. Neither Ravi nor I was prepared to disturb the status quo but surely — as we often justified to ourselves — we deserved the personal happiness that we gave each other. It was a fulfillment that actually made us happier and more compassionate providers in our respective families. It made sense to our lives and yet did not harm those we cared for.

Ravi and I met at our secret home about thrice a week and at these times shared moments of pure ecstasy with each other on the six-by-four-feet bed. That was real love-making, not the helpless and guilt-ridden experience I had earlier thought it was all about. To tell the truth, it was only these moments of our secret lives that had made the grind of the last twenty years, so much easier to bear.

Ravi's wife knew about us but she probably didn't care less. Ravi hadn't told their son about us. Just as I did not dare tell Biji nor Amala. Sometimes over the years, I often had a momentary feeling that Biji suspected something (a mother's instinct?). But soon enough the feeling would always pass out. And Amala? I would die a thousand deaths at the very thought of telling her! Though I knew that one day I would have to.

She was pure, fragile, and so very innocent. She thought the world of me and Biji and for her we could do no wrong. She knew of all the hardships I'd been through but knew nothing of my joys.

As a child, Amala often told me that she would look after us and make us so happy that we'd forget all the hardships we had ever faced. I must confess that I enjoyed wearing the mantle of martyr that the world had put like an ornament on me. I revelled in the image of the 'sacrificing all for your happiness' role that I played for Amala. Many a time I thought of telling her about my true relationship with Ravi, but the fear that my image would crumble in her eyes if I did that prevented me from doing so.

At other times, the fear of her getting to know elsehow and rejecting me because of it, was so overwhelming that I would decide to call it quits with Ravi. I would come to the entrance of our love-nest, mentally prepared to bid it goodbye forever. But having crossed that threshold, it would become impossible to turn back just then.

I would look at Ravi's smiling visage, and sit beside him. The lines I had rehearsed in my head would go asunder. Ravi had an uncanny way of finding out exactly what was going on in my mind, without me having to explain too much. And he consistently always succeeded in making me change my mind.

I remember the last time I was feeling this way. Ravi sat me down on the mattress. He removed my glasses and put them aside. He cradled my head against his chest and stroked my head — as if he were consoling a child. I was feeling so mixed up at that time. One moment I was like a child, soaking in the comfort of a parent's bosom and then, in the very next moment, I transformed from child to woman. A woman whose every nerve was alive, throbbing and pulsating to the touch of her man.

I had never been able to figure out why I always turned to putty in Ravi's hands. Maybe he was an exceptionally good lover. Maybe I was too ready, and too vulnerable to the only man that I had ever loved. Ultimately I stopped trying to attempt to give up my feelings for him.

It was by last summer that I was finally learning to enjoy the best of both worlds. I told myself that since Amala was by now a most understanding and mature girl I should soon be able to tell her all about Ravi. Little did I know at that time that my dreams of a friendship with my daughter were never to be.

Last summer Amala fell in love. Nitish was ten years older than her and he worked in the same office that Amala took up her summer job. I remember the day. It was, as I later learnt, their first date and she had agreed to go out with him for dinner without telling us, Biji or me. It seemed so innocent when I think of it now — so right for her to be doing such a thing at her age. But so horribly wrong to discover that her own parent had been up to much worse.

There she was looking into Nitish's eyes, talking perhaps of love, dreams and a future. And in the next moment she suddenly saw me clasping Ravi's hand. For me, too, it was unusual to concede to such a public display of affection, but it was this rare occassion when Ravi had insisted that we celebrate our fifteen years of togetherness at that restaurant.

Amala's world crashed and so did mine. Once she knew what Ravi meant to me, I had to give her all the details. The hypocrisy of my stand crushed her. There was just no way that she could accept my double standards. She did not believe that I had not wronged his family, or mine.

"I was prepared to fight my natural urges and dreams of marriage just so that I need never have to leave you, and that's what I'd been telling Nitish at that time. I wanted to spend my life taking care of you. But now I see that you have other people who do that and also give you what I can never give. You do not need me," was all that she had said tersely. And her words were indeed a portent of the future course of our relationship.

A few days later Amala came home with Nitish, informing Biji and me that they had just been through a court marriage. They were leaving within the week for Bombay where Nitish had found a challenging job.

Biji and I were stunned. There had been no reason for her to do it this way, for we would have accepted anyone whom she wished to marry. In any case Nitish did seem like a nice person and was also genuinely in love with her. But Amala did this just to spite me and I could not defend myself in front of Biji who was completely unaware of what had transpired between us.

And in spite of that Biji, in any case, held me to blame. In the true tradition of the partial grandmother, she felt that I had gone wrong somewhere for my daughter to have done this, the way she did.

"You have failed to be her friend," Biji had said accusingly.

I accepted her verdict. Yes of course I had gone wrong — only much more wrong than Biji could ever imagine. So very wrong that I had lost the right as a parent to point out my child's mistake or even to voice my protest against it. I suspect that Amala knew this and was enjoying hurting me, even as she was hurting herself.

It's been a year since Amala left. Gradually I stopped meeting Ravi and even left my job with his company. It was not because I stopped loving him — if anything I love and miss him more than ever before, after Amala left us. But soon after Amala's departure, even though she was no longer in the same city, each time I'd meet him I'd feel as if I was somehow hurting her all over again.

Ravi was dejected but he accepted my decision. The women in his life, he had remarked sadly that day, had always taken the decisions about their relationship and he had always had to go along. First Ketaki had done it, and now I had.

My Amala was a married woman now. My little girl who had never known a man before she wed — not a father, not even a brother — was now a woman. I'd often worried on that count and hoped that our similar backgrounds wouldn't lead to similar fates. But there had been no other option but to let go. There was no use worrying.

I wrote to Amala several times after she left. She would reply but did not tell me much about how she was doing. Every reply from her was evidence of the battle waging within her. A few lines that she would write to me would

sound like the Amala of old — as if nothing had gone wrong between us. Reading these my heart would skip a beat as I would imagine that she had finally forgiven me and was going to give me a peep into her life.

But in the very next paragraph she would be on guard and terse again. Could I hope that the first Amala would one day break free of the shackles that the second Amala had bound her with? I could only hope that time would heal and that this time when she saw me, that it would happen. Dare I hope?

PART 3

Achala put down her pen. It was past 5 o'clock in the morning.

Fifty years, five hours. Or fifty years in five hours, that she had just penned.

Both time-frames were in place. They were the long and short of time and of life itself. She looked at Biji stirring with the new lease of life that she had got.

Soon Biji would regain consciousness. Her eyes would most certainly search for Amala — pining for the person who had certainly contributed her mite to the stroke she had suffered two days ago.

Achala had called up Bombay soon after Biji had been admitted to hospital. In the dead of night Nitish had picked up the phone. He had sounded a bit strained when he had told Achala that he would 'pass on the message to Amala', instead of calling Amala to the phone. Perhaps Amala may not have wanted to come to the phone or maybe he was just being protective.

Achala had been expecting all through these last two days for Amala to come. Despite all that had happened with her, she must most certainly have been concerned about Biji even if she had stopped caring about her. For this was Biji's second attack after her bypass surgery and Amala was well aware of the threat to Biji's life during her earlier hospitalisation. There was certainly something mysterious and worrisome about Amala not having come to see Biji so far.

With the first chirping and twittering of the birds came the sounds of life stirring in the hospital corridor. The swish-swoosh sound of huge thread mops, the faint but comforting smell of tea brewing in the pantry, the sounds of buckets filling up with water in the adjoining bathrooms — all heralding the beginning of another day of healing.

Suddenly there was a sharp knock on the door of Biji's room and Achala rushed to open it. The plump matron walked inside. Surely it was premature for Biji to be given a sponge bath today, thought Achala as she let her in. The matron entered and shut the door behind her.

"Madam, there is something strange going on," she told Achala.

"Since last night a young girl has been sitting on the bench outside. She said she was related to the patient in this room so we allowed her to come in even though it was past visiting hours. But this morning as I passed through the corridor I found that she is still sitting crouched on the bench. She looks ill and very scared. Please tell us whether you know her or else I'll have to inform security," she continued.

Before the matron could complete her sentence Achala had rushed out. There, crouched on the bench, she saw the huddled figure of Amala. She looked pale as a ghost, and as haunted as an animal in the captivity of its own mind. She had lost a lot of weight and her usually kohl-rimmed eyes now looked so sunken. As she saw Achala rush towards her, Amala started to weep, her body racked and heaved as she sobbed.

Achala hugged her as she sat crouched on the bench. Amala buried her face in the pleats of her mother's sari, feeling its warmth as she used to when she was a little girl. Achala led her inside Biji's room as the matron was bewildered at the scene.

Achala wanted to hold Amala tight but a strange fear prevented her from doing so. She guided Amala to sit on the lone chair in the room, and then went to sit across her on the low stool.

"What's the matter Amala? Why did you not come in earlier? Do you still hate me or were you afraid that Biji....?"

"I don't know why I did not come in. But I know that I love you Ma and I need you..... " she whispered, extending her hand to stroke Biji's emaciated feet. "I love you both," she said in a hoarse whisper.

"What's wrong my child?" asked Achala shaking Amala's knees in fear.

"I have sinned, Ma. I think it was God's way of punishing me for having judged you. I don't know why I did it, Ma," she cried.

"What have you done?" asked Achala, concerned, but afraid of being betrayed by the sound of her own voice, actually wondering and hoping that her sympathy was truly warranted.

"I left Nitish a month ago. Ma, I thought I didn't get the love I was looking for from him and.... and I found it in Rahul ... or so I had thought at that time. I have been living with Rahul this past month. Living in sin. But even with Rahul things are not what I thought they would be. I wronged Nitish. I've made a mess of my life and now I have nowhere to go?" her words poured out disjointed and scattered as her thoughts.

"How did you get to know about Biji?" Achala queried strangely relieved at Amala's explanation.

"Nitish rang me up the day before yesterday at Rahul's house and told me about Biji. I left Bombay yesterday. Rahul did not even care to drop me to the airport. His look was almost a message to me that I was not really welcome to return. I guess my emotional needs were too much for him to bear — he was looking for something else. I have been a fool, an utter fool. Rahul didn't want my emotions, he only wanted me. And once he got me, it was all over. Ma, I really wronged Nitish. I found him too boring and staid but the truth is that when I was with him I always felt that there was someone to take care of me. I have hurt him and therefore God has punished me........".

"I am there for you Amala. I have being waiting so long to be able to take care of you," said Achala.

"But I have no right to expect that now. I have hurt you too haven't I?" asked Amala. "I've hurt you so much."

"One hurts those whom one loves. But tell me Amala, do you still love Nitish?"

"More than ever before. I know that I sound most selfish, but the truth is that I love and value him more than ever before. But now I know that it's too late," she admitted.

"You will not lose him. I will try my best to see that you don't. If you lose him now, I know that you'll lose yourself. Your identity will disintegrate... some bits will remain with you while others will be blown away by the wind; just as grains of sand in the desert are. Every woman is like sand. It is fate that gives her a desert, or the sea, as her companion. So her man is either as restless as the wind or as placid as water. I was destined to be in the desert, but I will take you to your sea, my child," said Achala, stroking Amala's knees.

There was a knock on the door. This time it woke up Biji who stared sideways at the entrance as if expecting someone there, completely missing to look at Achala and Amala standing close by.

Achala opened the door and stared in surprise at Nitish. The disbelief writ large on Amala's face slowly turned into belief as he walked with serene steps towards her.

"How are you Amala?" he asked and the lines on her overwrought face melted away.

"I'm all right Nitish... I've learnt so much about life and love recently. But I know that it's too late now to make amends for what I've done."

"It's not late — it's never too late to understand and forgive in love," said Nitish.

"You mean its possible for you to accept me after all that...?" asked Amala, disbelief returning to her like a bad penny once again.

"It's not that I can't accept you again. But even if I do, what happened to you some time ago will happen again, unless..." said Nitish looking her in the eye.

"Unless you accept and face up to something you are still avoiding..." he said softly, but firmly.

Nitish held Amala's hand and led her towards the door as Biji's furtive, whine-like pleas reached their ears. Nitish paused and turned to look at Biji. For the sake of her weak ears he reassured her in a particularly loud voice "Don't worry Biji, I'm coming back. I'm just going to get someone who should have been here right through. Just coming back Biji."

Biji's plaints stopped miraculously at this male command, as Achala and Amala both looked at Nitish's resolute face.

"There is someone whom you have to accept, before you expect me to accept you," he explained. "A person who is as important to your family as I am... and today I've brought him here with me," said Nitish as he opened the door of Biji's room and led Amala to the beginning of a long corridor.

There at the far end, seated on the same bench on which Amala had crouched all night, sat Ravi.

"Go Amala, go and accept him with all your heart. If you can do that you will be able to love yourself... and only then will my love be able to reach you. Only then will you truly be able to love me Amala. Me or anyone else. Believe me Amala, for once believe me," said Nitish.

"I do" whispered Amala.

Ravi stood up and looked at Amala, in a strange way able and yet unable to meet her stare. Amala walked towards him with clouded eyes. She folded her hands and cried, "I'm sorry Ravi uncle, really sorry."

Ravi held her drooping shoulders and then put her head on his chest, patting her head as she wept, so drained and comforted that she didn't want anything to stop or change this moment. But change it still did, with the sound of Nitish's voice. "It looks as if Biji connived with fate to cause her illness — an illness that has healed us all today."

They all walked back towards Biji's room where Achala met them, her eyes dry and lips unable to stop smiling. They went past her and close to Biji's bed. Biji's eyes were now wide open.

Biji's face looked beatific, her wrinkles went deeper into her skin as she attempted to smile. Her eyes were twinkling, seeming to speak a thousand words. She signalled to Achala who walked towards her from the far end of the room.

Achala put her ears close to Biji's mouth. "Guineas" Biji whispered hoarsely.

"They are there Biji. They are still tied in your chunni. No one has taken them," said Achala sounding exasperated as she reassured Biji, like she were talking to a child.

"I want to hold the guineas," said Biji firmly, her hoarse voice cracking but firm.

Achala was surprised at Biji's instructions but proceeded to fulfill her wish. She opened Biji's chunni knot and placed the two guineas in her left palm. Biji shut her eyes and closed her palm as to feel the familiar and comforting presence of the guineas one last time. Then, as though satiated, she opened her eyes again.

"Ravi beta," she whispered. Ravi bent forward to come closer to her. She placed one guinea in his hand. Ravi looked nonplussed as Achala looked on with tears of relief in her eyes.

"Nitish puttar," said Biji, as she beckoned him. He stared bewildered, and then hesitantly walked towards Biji. She placed the second guinea in his palm.

"God bless you all. Now I can finally sleep in peace and talk to Bauji in my dreams," she said as she sighed and shut her tired eyes.

11

A Decision at Last

A Decision at Last

"It has become a part of your cultural DNA, you suffer from an almost pathological wish to be dominated." Shekhar had yelled in disgust at Kajol, a few months after they were married. She had broken out into a fit of giggles at this analysis. Such a complete gender role reversal in their thought processes. Her husband, Shekhar, was an ardent votary of women's empowerment and to that end, in their early years of marriage had often encouraged her to try and take a lot of decisions on her own. But she had simply refused to heed his wishes.

It was not that Kajol hadn't tried. But time and again she had realised that she was simply helpless in her limitations. The more choices Kajol had, the more bewildered she became. The moment she was faced with a decision to make, it was as though she could see in her line of vision, a series of lanes and alleys fusing and merging into one another. She felt like a magnet being pulled in so many directions at the same time. And so Kajol always ended up begging Shekhar to decide for her. It made life so much easier and lighter.... She always felt like a soaring bird the moment she shifted the awesome responsibility of decision making to him.

Over the years, of course, there had been some improvement. In the smaller issues of life, from not deciding at all, it had at least graduated to Kajol helping certain decisions being made. What outfit to wear for the Sharmas' anniversary party, what new dishes to order from the menu of their favourite restaurants, whether the children ought to join a new extra curricular activity or not, she had at least started to state her views. But even then, it was finally, always, his call. And she was relieved and thanked God for that.

Shekhar often complained to her that though she performed all the duties of being a wife and mother satisfactorily, he worried for her. She was like a third child for him; loving, innocent but someone who simply refused to grow up. Shekhar had imagined a more tough and equal life partner, like what his mother had been to his father. But gradually Shekhar and Kajol both got used to her indecisiveness, as loving partners in a marriage usually get used to each other's idiosyncrasies. Because it was also true that despite all the notions of an equal partnership, the best marriages and partnership are those in which one partner accepts the superior wisdom of the other on one issue or the other. One thinks and decides, the other executes, and peace and happiness actually reigns in most such homes.

In any case Shekhar always thought right. Kajol could not remember any one time in these ten years when they had regretted any decision that he had taken. When he was so blessed while she was not, how did it matter that it was he who always decided, she had told a still-dissatisfied Shekhar often.

"It's important to have an opinion, and a viewpoint... even if it sometimes proves to be wrong. How long will you depend on me to take all the decisions about our life?" he had asked just the previous week, irritated when he had to decide the brand of the washing machine that they were planning to buy.

"Forever," Kajol had said and given him a hug. Thankfully, once more he had been assuaged. Ironical, but this was exactly what Kajol felt, although deep in her heart she knew, that his concern was genuine and in the fitness of things.

She thought things would soon become normal again and Shekhar wouldn't be irritated with her on this issue. But that afternoon when he came home early from work, with a plan to take the family for a surprise weekend vacation, he asked her to try and decide where they should go.

"Anywhere," she said smiling at him, hoping it would work as usual.

Shekhar seemed irritated as he disentangled himself from her arms. "It's not funny," he said. "There's something seriously wrong with you Kajol."

"Oh Shekhar, not again... I thought we had worked this out between us," Kajol said.

"What's the problem Kajol? Does it take the strength of Bhim or the wisdom of Arjun to decide whether we should go to Mahableshwar for the weekend or just go upto Marve. Just forget it. I'll wait for the kids to come from school and tell me. Today I had actually wanted to surprise them... just bundle them into the car and not tell them where we were going... but never mind now." Shekhar was irritated and looked preoccupied as he stirred the soup in the bowl.

"But why don't you decide like always, Shekhar. We'll go anywhere. The idea is to take this weekend break and be together. Why are you making such a fuss this time Shekhar?" asked Kajol.

"Why don't you understand Kajol. I feel very guilty always deciding for everyone. Anyway, let the kids come home and decide... I want that they should start thinking for themselves from the right age, otherwise they'll end up like you have. And what's more, they might never be able to change their minds and habits later, just as you haven't been able to," he said bitterly.

"Mahabaleshwar!" blurted Kajol as Shekhar almost scalded his tongue with the first spoon of soup that he put into his mouth. "I've decided that we should go to Mahableshwar," she said.

Shekhar got up from his chair and took Kajol off hers. He twirled her around as she giggled. Jai and Tanu walked in just then and stared in disbelief, then abandoned their satchels and joined in.

In no time at all suitcases were packed and they hit the road. It was like a scene in the movies. The romantic drizzle... miles of fields that looked like freshly painted greens... the car deck blaring "You fill up my senses..." with two beautiful children dozing in the backseat. And then like a proverbial twist in a screen tale, the car skidding to avoid a speeding truck in front... the muffled implosion of metal bodies colliding, the scrunch of twisting steel.

Shekhar had slumped over the steering wheel after their car had rammed into a tree. Jai and Tanu were unscathed and Kajol was shaken and bruised. But Shekhar now clung on to life only with the help of the life support machine.

Kajol looked with glazed eyes at Shekhar sleeping peacefully. The oxygen mask was over his mouth... tubes all over his arm... the ECG machine connected to his chest. The hospital sheet covered him upto his ribs and the caked lines of mud and dried blood in his hair.

Kajol stared numbly at him as she stood by his side. It was she who had decided to come to Mahableshwar and the decision had gone so wrong. So very wrong. This was exactly why she always hated taking decisions... but no one had ever understood how justified she was. This time even Shekhar hadn't.

"Have you taken a decision yet?"

Kajol nearly jumped out of her skin. No, it wasn't Shekhar

asking.

Kajol turned around. It was Dr Verma. "I know Ma'am, this is a very tough decision.... but this isn't getting anyone anywhere. We wouldn't be suggesting this, if there was even the faintest chance of recovery. Your husband is in coma, he's only technically alive... only due to these machines.... I've seen plenty of such cases and, believe me, they almost never pull out. Even if they do, there is serious brain damage. Either way, it is traumatic for the family... Only you can give us permission to pull off life support..." the doctor continued.

Another decision? How could Kajol tell them she could not take this decision? No she certainly could not, she simply could not.

Kajol finally broke down as she looked at Shekhar, "Don't let me go through this Shekhar. Help me Shekhar, help me," she cried. Tears flowed down her cheeks and more kept clouding her eyes, reducing the visage of the supine Shekhar to a mere blur. The tears seemed unending.... Shekhar had earlier, never been able to ignore them... they had always been her ultimate weapon. But now... he lay completely unaffected. But wait... didn't he...??

Yes... miracle of miracles.... he seemed to be responding!! Kajol wiped her eyes quickly... she couldn't be wrong... she was sure that she saw Shekar's hand move. She rushed to tell the doctor.... A miracle... it must be a miracle!

The doctor conceded that it had been a miracle all right. Shekhar's hand had jerked at an angle that had pulled off the oxygen mask and, two gasps later, he was gone.

He had taken the decision for her yet another time.

12

Family Ties

Family Ties

Only Vijayalakshmi Nair knew exactly how difficult this journey had actually been. She was a hundred per cent certain that none of her twenty-nine graduating batchmates at Kerala's first business school could ever dream of where she really came from. To them, she was the urbane and cute Lux that she had so meticulously projected herself as, in these last two years.

It was all very well to read and admire rags-to-riches or country bumpkin-to-graduate stories in the newspapers. But Lux firmly believed that while she was still here studying, if her friends did indeed find out her background, they'd be both embarrassed and disdainful about accepting her as easily as they did. But yes, one day in the future Lux would definitely tell her story. Then, she was sure that there would be only admiration for both her and her family, not only from people at large but also from her peers. It would only be then that they would look at the situation from the right perspective which would come with the passage of time.

Lux knew that such a day was finally not very far away now. After her graduation ceremony today, she would be leaving for Bombay right away to take up that job in a multinational company there. She would then send for her parents from their village in Thekkady to live with her. She would gently groom them to presentable levels and later showcase their story to the outside world.

Lux straightened the collar of her shirt and smoothened the non-existent creases of her jacket. Ten minutes more to go for the ceremony. She took out the photograph of her parents from an envelope carefully kept in the jacket of her diary and looked at it. "Sorry Appa, sorry Amma... I did not inform you about the ceremony today. Because I know that if I had, you both would definitely have come."

"Of course I would have been happy to see you here. But the truth is that I would also have been unhappy in another sense. I know that everyone here would have silently sniggered at the sight of both of you — Appa, your dhoti and turban... Amma your coarse saree and plastic chappals unable to hide the mud-filled cracks in your heels. How would the people here accept and understand you? So I hope that you will understand instead."

The smell of coconut oil from Amma's hair and the sour odour of sweat from Appa's armpits — they were smells that meant the world to her. But here, in a hall full of three-piece-suit clad fathers and chiffon-clad mothers weighed down with pearls, they would have been the object of suppressed ridicule. That was the reason that Lux had not even told them about today though it was the culmination of all their dreams — their dreams for her which were also their only dreams.

Appa and Amma always taught her never to judge anyone by his or her outward appearance. She had tried not to initially but they had no idea how different the world was today.

"Someday I will make it up to both of them for today. I'll make up to Appa for the years of sowing, reaping and starving that he did to send me here. And the tons of spices Amma pounded for the traders until her hands turned red, after all her housework was done. I know that she did this to send me my pocket money," thought Lux as her eyes clouded.

"I always asked, and you always gave. Today I ask from you once again.... Give me your blessings Appa... your blessings Amma," said Lux aloud as she lovingly stroked the black and white picture of her stiffly-posing parents, and then put it back in its envelope. She was getting late.

She made her way to her allotted seat in the first row among all her batchmates. In the row behind sat the staff and behind them, the fifty-odd parents of the proud graduates. The speeches began in earnest but there was a disturbance a few minutes later near the entrance.

Lux turned to look there. Her heart sank. There stood Appa and Amma... just as she had visualised them a few minutes earlier as she had stared at their picture in her room. They were convincing the security guard in Malayalam that they had the Principal's invitation to be here. The uncomprehending guard looked them up and down and then examined the invitation. He reluctantly signaled them to join in the audience, not wanting to disturb the proceedings any further.

All this while Lux had been transfixed to her seat, too frozen even to squirm. The Principal called out her name as the recipient of the Best Student Award for the year. Lux walked with heavy steps to the stage, looking at the audience from the corner of her worrying eyes. Appa and Amma were clapping loudly, their smiles extending from ear to ear. Lux accepted the award, but did not go back to her seat, choosing instead a place from where she could keep an eye on Appa and Amma. From where they couldn't see that she was doing so.

She settled down carefully, putting her medal into its case and the case into her trouser pocket. Then she looked discreetly behind. Appa and Amma looked uncomfortable as they sensed so many eyes upon them. It also looked as if they had realised, that some of the twitters around had something to do with them. Lux saw Appa whispering something into Amma's ears. She silently prayed that they wouldn't do anything to embarrass her any further.

Lux saw Amma and Appa get up and walk to the entrance. This time the Principal, who had by now come off the podium, went towards them too. He looked confused as he spoke. "You must be Vijayalakshmi's parents?" he said, the forced warmth in his voice unable to override the look of slight contempt in his eyes as he looked at them from head to toe. "I had sent a special invitation to Vijayalakshmi's home since she was winning the Best Student Award," he said.

Lux could sit no more. She almost jumped out of her seat and then walked quickly towards the trio. She opened her mouth to explain but the voice of Appa beat her to it.

"No *Saar*... merely workers in Vijayalakshmi's parent's farm we are. Vijayalakshmi's Appa and Amma? They are in foreign land.... We only came to see her *Saar*... now we've seen... very nice *Saar*... all very nice.... Thank you very much *Saar*. *Namaskaram*."

Appa folded his hands and led Amma away quickly.

The muffled laughter and squeals of "How cute... how touching...!" in the hall caused Lux's eyes to well. She was afraid the tears would fall and was too conscious of the many eyes upon her, to be able to move her hand over her eyes to stem them.

"Vijayalakshmi, I think you ought to leave them to the gate, they are such sweet country folk. Just imagine, you're nothing to them and yet they came so far to see you," the Principal said, secretly relieved that they were not really Vijayalakshmi's parents.

"We city folk must learn from them...These rural people are so large hearted," he continued, shaking his head from side to side."

"But you Vijayalakshmi, where are your manners, my girl? Off you go behind them. Go on, see them off at the gate."

"Yes Sir," said Lux as she walked with great relief behind Appa and Amma.

13

Turning Point

Turning Point

Ajoy was trying to lift his wife Shobha who had suddenly fainted before him. He had been complimenting her about her insight into human character, when it happened. Poor thing, she was not used to his praise. Perhaps it was just a fainting spell. As he lay Shobha on the divan and turned on the fan, Ajoy's mind raced over the events of the day.

Yes, he recalled standing outside Ms Sengupta's office in the morning...

"Ms Sengupta?"

"May I come in, Ms Sengupta?" Ajoy asked hesitantly, as he knocked at her cabin door.

"Come in," she answered.

From the tone of her voice itself, Ajoy knew that Ms Sengupta had answered him without the usual *joie de vivre* that had been characteristic of her mannerism, as well as her spirit.

Of course, Ajoy knew that she couldn't really be blamed for this. Not after what had happened at the office party last night.

"Damn Shobha," he thought for the nth time that morning, as he thought of his wife while entering Ms Sengupta's cabin. If only he could summon enough courage to tell her that he wanted out of this marriage. If only he had had those nerves of steel, then circumstances would not have brought him to a situation like the present. Where he stood wrecked with shame and regret over his wife's conduct, outside his colleague's door.

Ajoy bit his lip with hesitation, then finally walked up towards her. Ms Sengupta sat behind her table and looked at him silently for a moment. Then, with her hand still holding the pencil that she had been sketching with, she beckoned him to sit.

She looked even more beautiful when she was a trifle subdued like this, than when she was her usual chirpy self. Ajoy noticed that the kajal outlining her eyes never ever spilled out and transgressed its limits — like Shobha's often did. Almost as if the kajal had a mind of its own and decided not to, lest it detract any appeal from its beautiful subject. Ms Sengupta's lips, now hesitant to break into a smile, looked even more luscious as the perfectly-in-place black mole above her right lip quivered as she spoke.

She brushed aside her burgundy coloured hair. Ajoy could not help wondering as he settled into the seat opposite her, what kind of man could possibly leave a woman as gorgeous and lovely as Ms Sengupta.

It was a thought that had not struck him earlier as emphatically as it had at this moment. In an advertising agency like the one he worked in, it was not unusual for men to be working alongside divorced or single women, without bothering to find out why they were so. And yet today, the thought was bothering him like it had never before during the last one year that she had been his art designer.

He knew that it was Shobha who was responsible for this heightened awareness. Shobha, and the clear jealousy and hostility that she had displayed towards Ms Sengupta at the office party last night.

The incident had made Ajoy realise that Ms Sengupta's

sensuous charm and single status, made many more-ordinary women like Shobha very insecure.

"I'm very sorry about last night, Ms Sengupta. I don't know what came over Shobha to behave the way she did. I wish to apologise on her behalf," he said, wondering what more he could possibly say on the matter at this juncture.

"You've been calling me Ms Sengupta long enough Ajoy, call me Jaya," she said. "It's all right, you don't have to apologise. It's not the first time that this has happened to me. A lot of married women feel very threatened by their husband's single-women colleagues. It's something I have sensed very often in these last three years that I've been single and working. I can't say that it doesn't hurt or affect me at all — but I think I can handle it a lot better now than I used to earlier. Earlier I would be completely shattered, but look at me today. I'm fine and I'm back at work despite what happened yesterday," she explained softly.

Jaya was trying to be brave but Ajoy could see the sadness around her lips. How gracious she was being about the whole sorry episode. It was as if she epitomised all the feminine qualities that a woman could possibly possess. And to think that he hadn't noticed any of this through the entire year that they had been colleagues!

"I really don't know what to say — but I really feel so miserable Ms......er.. Jaya," Ajoy continued, wincing at his inability to find better words to express how he was feeling.

"Don't say anything more and don't feel miserable either. Let's not discuss this any further.... For me you're still the colleague that you were. And a nice one at that," she added. Her lips finally broke into a full smile. A smile, that as he had noticed earlier, went right up to her eyes.

The telephone rang and Jaya picked it up. She started to

chat with a friend. Ajoy muttered a soft goodbye and left the cabin.

Somehow, Jaya's brave smile only made him feel much worse than the righteous tantrum that he had expected from her. He simply had to do something more than just accept Jaya's gracious forgiveness, a forgiveness that had overwhelmed him completely.

Ajoy had seen only the contrary tendencies in his wife, Shobha. She had had such an easy life compared to Jaya. He had treated her well, unlike how Jaya's husband had probably treated her. She was also financially secure and actually revelled in Ajoy's status in social circles, more than he himself felt comfortable doing. Yet, she always found fault in others, especially if they were women. There was always some deep, mysterious reason why she believed that everybody else had a better deal in life than her. Of course, this had nothing to do with her own self — nature and destiny, according to her, always conspired to give an advantage to others. Psychologists called that a persecution complex.

It was this attitude that had prompted her to go up to Jaya the previous evening and acerbically comment that single women like her had no respect for institutions like marriage and family. She had made it worse by saying that more than other women, those having had broken marriages themselves thought nothing of breaking up the marriages of decent, happily married women.

It had started out as an academic discussion but developed into a personalised conversation. Given Shobha's tendencies to dominate, a monologue would be a more apt term to describe what that interaction had been all about. And God alone knew what else Shobha had said to Jaya apart from this, what a stunned Ajoy had heard in bits and pieces, while he had had to make polite conversation with one of their clients. But suffice it to say that Jaya, not being the sort to get defensive in the face of Shobha's aggressive posturing, had made a dignified exit from the party all due to her.

Ajoy had berated Shobha about it at home the previous night. Of course Shobha had said that she was talking 'general truths', and that it was Jaya's guilty conscience that had made her smart from Shobha's comments. She had closed the argument with Ajoy by saying that, in any case, vain women like Jaya 'deserved' what they got. And that one day Ajoy would realise how much insight she had into the darker truths of human character.

Ajoy had realised that it was no use arguing with Shobha. She was just not the kind of person who would ever accept that she had done any wrong. And in recent months she was only getting worse, picking on people she had little to do with and becoming not just difficult to live with, but increasingly also a social embarrassment.

Ajoy knew that the situation was getting beyond repair. He would sooner or later have to separate from her, for he could not imagine being able to put up with this all his life. He had already started avoiding spending time with Shobha, and knew that sooner or later he would have to muster the nerves to tell her that he wanted out of the marriage. It was just that he would need to develop nerves of steel to issue the ultimatum to her and be able to handle its aftermath. But unfortunately he hadn't the faintest idea how to develop these steel nerves.

Right now, of course, he must first repair the latest damage that Shobha had done. Jaya had handled all this with such rare dignity that Ajoy was determined it would not go unappreciated. He sat at his desk all day, planning his evening trip to Jaya's house armed with an apology card, flowers and what was he definitely knew was her defining and favourite perfume — Anais Anais.

It was a comforting thought to plan this trip. And it was even more cathartic to chose the right bouquet, the right shade of wrapping paper for the bottle of perfume, and write the apology card all of which he finally came armed with at Jaya's door late that evening.

Jaya was overwhelmed that he had taken so much trouble and simply insisted that he stay on for dinner — an invitation that he was actually very happy to accept. For it meant that he would get to spend one more evening away from Shobha.

It had the class of a wine-and-roses affair — never mind if what followed, was only cheese sandwiches and instant soup. But it was food laced with the aphrodisiac of the attraction and understanding that two misunderstood people had found in each other that evening.

Ajoy found Jaya in his arms, and it took him some time to believe that she really was there. He wondered how he had mustered the courage to make the first move... He had never thought he was capable of wearing his heart on his sleeve, or of being able to make his feelings known for any woman. And least of all to a woman such as Jaya, who was the epitome of elegance. What would have happened if something had gone wrong... or if she had not reciprocated his feelings? How would he have faced her the next day? He dreaded these thoughts. But here she was, and she was reluctant to let go of him. And that was all what mattered.

Ajoy could feel Jaya responding to him. She matched him stride for stride. Yes, more than anything else, after many years, Ajoy enjoyed the feeling of controlling a woman physically and emotionally. He felt confident, like a man.

Much later, as he stood on his own doorstep, Ajoy felt a cocktail of emotions coursing through him. Should he feel guilty? Hadn't Shobha brought this upon herself? Frankly, did he feel anything for Shobha? Yet, she was his wife and how could he have done this to her... His head was in a whirl when the door was opened by Shobha, who sized him from head to foot and launched into a tirade even before he crossed the lintel.

But this time Ajoy did not back off. He wanted to test his manliness again. What a great feeling it would be for his perpetually crushed ego if he were to score over Shobha? He stared at her hard and, and in a gesture he had never tried on Shobha before, raised his forefinger as a warning to her to stop. Shobha was startled.

Then, in a low voice he said. "You were right Shobha, absolutely right. Single women like Jaya really do not respect marriage. How easily they entrap stupid men like myself with their charm and wit. But I love being trapped... and I will always remember your insight into the darker truths of human character."

That was when Shobha collapsed on the pile carpet...

14

The Final Act

The Final Act

"Sir is very serious, Mrs Das It is better if you come with Rahulji. We are all waiting for you both," said Nair, his voice quivering as he spoke. Chhaya heard the clicking sound of the phone being disconnected at the other end. Nair had put it down before she could ask any more questions. He was probably scared of the truth coming out in an emotional breakdown, if he spoke any more.

But even without his admittance, it was clear to Chhaya that her husband Amarendra was no more. She knew that this heart attack at fifty-six, in the middle of dictating notes to his faithful secretary Nair, had felled him. Perhaps it was just the kind of end he would himself have wanted — to die with his boots on and with as little emotion and in as clinical a manner as he had lived his life. Like the battery running out of some electronic equipment. At least the fact that he had a heart attack proved that he had a heart, thought Chhaya for that certainly wasn't the faintest of impressions that she had in all these years of being his wife.

It was certainly mean for her to be thinking this way, at a time like this. Chhaya sat on the settee beside the telephone. It was a moment that she had imagined and relived in her mind umpteen times in these last twenty-five years.

She had often wondered how it would finally happen, how they would bring his body home and how she would behave through all that would follow. Now that moment had finally come. It was the time to put up the last act of the marriage drama that she had been starring in for a quarter century. But the problem was that like the finale of any good drama it would have to be a most convincing display of histrionics. Because all these years she had only had to put up a show for a few people around her — but this she knew, was going to be the most trying performance yet. The 'part' of her life, to be played at the time of his death. Today Chhaya felt like an amateur actress nervous at the prospect of facing a big audience for the first time.

Chhaya recalled the numerous times that she had been left alone to brood in their bedroom after a particularly bad fight with Amarendra. As soon as she would hear his car leave the drive-way after the fight, she would bolt the bedroom door from inside. Then she would sit in front of the dressing table mirror for a few cathartic moments. She would contort her face into possible expressions of grief at the imagined passing away of Amarendra. A couple of times she had genuinely tried to cry — to feel grief at his imagined death, perhaps by remembering the few times that he had been good to her.

But to summon enough reasons to miss him had always proved tough, actually nearly impossible for her. Alarmed at the cactus-like state of her emotions she had experimented with glycerine, onion juice, even the eucalyptus-based cold rub around her eyes, but they had succeeded in activating her tear glands just for a very brief while. They would not be able to help her cry at the crucial time, for each of them were dead give-aways by virtue of their sight or smell. So this problem had gradually become one that remained unresolved, as did all other issues that connected Amarendra to her.

Why was she so sure that he would die suddenly? And that he would die sooner than her? Chhaya had asked herself these questions many times. She herself did not know why she was so sure that he would. While she had wished him dead many times, she had never even remotely thought of plotting his murder. The idea of his death remained only a fantasy, bordering on wishful thinking, on her part.

Was this just a woman's gut feeling? Perhaps. But it was a gut feeling backed by the logic of reasoning. Amarendra did not keep very good health. His heavy boozing and smoking, his middle-age paunch, his absolute apathy towards his diabetic condition and his philandering were all contributory factors. Most of all was the fact that he did not even believe in resolving conflicts. All of this was bound to lead to the end. And it was also bound to be sooner rather than later.

The time bomb had finally gone off today. And for Chhaya, the moment to be reckoned with was here. Chhaya called out to her son, Rahul. Twenty-three year old Rahul, who was the one good thing that had come out of her marriage to Amarendra.

Rahul was a protective son. He would not hear of taking her to hospital just then. "Let me take charge," he said, putting his arm around her.

"I'll call you from there and let you know the situation," he continued perhaps sensing that she was not quite ready for what had not yet been confirmed, even as he himself showed an expression that clearly stated that he knew that his dad was probably more than 'very serious'.

Chhaya agreed because she knew that she needed time to prepare. Time to resolve, more than anything else — the issue of tears. Until now, every conflict that she had had with Amarendra was only hers to resolve. Hers to resolve in whichever way she wanted to. Today would be a public performance. She was finally going to be in control of herself and of the proceedings that were going to follow, indeed of the remainder of her whole life. It was an awesome and exhilarating feeling, one that she had not experienced in a long long time. And yet to enable herself to savour it forever, she would first have to pretend to be the brave and grief-stricken wife.

Chhaya walked back slowly to her bedroom. She looked at the king-size bed bought twenty-five years ago along with so many other upper class accessories that they had purchased when they had shifted into this huge flat. Chhaya pictured Amarendra and herself as they had lain beside each other night after night on either side of the bed — its ample space thankfully providing a safe distance between them.

Some nights of course she had been 'taken' in those early days. Merely aberrations before Amarendra and she would both assume their normal positions on either side of the bed again.

Two years after some such aberrations Rahul had been born. He had so conveniently come to occupy the space between them that he actually succeeded in moving each of them somewhat away from the sides of the bed and more towards its centre, where he slept.

This was the only distance that Rahul ever succeeded in bridging between his parents.

He had slept between them until he was ten years old. By then it was almost certain that Chhaya would never need contraception again. By now Amarendra did not even 'need' her sometimes, as he did in the first few years of marriage. She had grown plump and dumpy. While earlier she had known that she was not someone he could really 'show off' at the social dos that he attended, now, as he had caustically commented, she wasn't someone he could even merely 'show'.

There were so many others to fulfill his various needs and she had more or less accepted it this way. He didn't need her and he made that very obvious to her.

Chhaya looked at herself in the dressing table mirror. It was the same mirror into which she had tested all those crying experiments. Her face was frozen now, and seemed incapable of any kind of expression. She found it difficult to meet her own eyes in her reflection in the mirror. She looked at the rest of her, cold misshapen and dull. Yes, it was what stared back at her from the mirror that was the real reason, and not Rahul, that she had not left Amarendra when love had left them.

Who else would have her now? She had grown so used to the trappings and tags that being Amarendra's wife, so easily accorded her. She was a woman of limited looks and talents and therefore had few options. It made more sense to stay on in the marriage, and therefore very long ago Chhaya had made up her mind to heed her instinct for survival.

In fact, survival as an art form was something that she had learnt from Amarendra. She had learnt from him how to exist purely at the physical level. This was also in a way the greatest nirvana of all; a kind of worldly preparation for the ultimate release of the soul.

And so each day in these last few years had been spent eating, sleeping, bathing, drinking, cleaning, breathing and just being — daily chores that had been elevated to a state of meditation.

For Chhaya this meditation was disturbed only by all the emotions that motherhood had clawed out of her. Rahul's hugs and his tears, his wants and his fears, they consumed her days at first. Then, as he grew, they merely punctuated the silences in an otherwise meditative day. And in these last few years they appeared only like the rare rainbow on the colourless horizon of her existence. The truth was that now Rahul did not need her in the manner that he did as a child.

In these last few years Chhaya had grown restive again. Like a sage unable to meditate anymore, she was full of questions addressed to herself, that she had earlier put to sleep in the cosy lap of her practical wisdom. Questions about her whole life and its significance. A life now tired of its endless journey, on a road where there were no turns at all. Until now. Until this strange moment that had descended upon them all.

Chhaya sat still on the dressing table stool. Even through the closed door she could hear the voices of so many people now. They had obviously been let in by the bewildered family retainer Shankar.

"No, No, No, we can't let her remain inside. Never mind protocol at a time like this, we must go and get her from her bedroom." That was definitely the voice of Mrs Nair. Chhaya felt the voices coming closer and closer to the bedroom door.

" It's all right. After all Rahul asked us all to take charge and moreover to take particular care of his mother," said another voice.

"Let's go to her, it's just not right to leave her to her own grief and shock. Sometimes people do dangerous things at such times, they can even harm themselves if they get too dazed by grief," Mrs Nair exclaimed, her voice full of concern as she proceeded to push open the door.

And as the door burst open at that moment, half-a-dozen women, arms outstretched, walked towards a frozen Chhaya.

"Oh my dear!" wailed Mrs Nair. Then, as if on cue, the others joined in with each of their cries registering different decibel levels. Mrs Nair hugged Chhaya tightly. Chhaya's face fell and she felt her heart sink as she heard the sounds of commotion in the hall outside and the din of car doors opening and closing with rapidity in the courtyard. The moment was finally upon her — there was just no way that it could be wished away any longer. But as Chhaya realised to her horror, she was still not yet prepared to face things.

Each of the women now proceeded to hug her and each of them by turn said a few words to her. Chhaya seemed to absorb it all like a zombie, stony-eyed and unmoved.

"She's still in shock," she heard someone whispering close to her.

"He was such a nice man. Never harmed a fly. I pray for his soul to rest in peace and in heaven," said another. Chhaya's eyes were still dry.

The women led her, supporting her hands and her back, as if she was an invalid, into the hall.

Chhaya noticed with amazement how quickly the furniture and carpets had all been moved to the sides of the hall. How quickly everything had been organised to accommodate the farewell to the master of this home. Her gaze fell upon Rahul, Nair and the others as they entered through the front door holding the poles of the stretcher with Amarendra's body on it. She then saw them lower the stretcher to the ground.

Rahul was now crying aloud. He cradled his father's head in his hand as the others then proceeded to help in placing Amarendra's body on the ground.

Men of all shapes and sizes dressed in differing hues of white, more or less surrounded Amarendra and blocked her view. Then after what seemed like eternity she was slowly led further and further towards him, and her torso was gently pushed to bend so that she could kneel beside his body.

Chhaya looked at Amarendra's face. The face of the man that she had grown to hate. It was the first time in years that she was looking at him so closely. Somehow, she hadn't imagined that his face would be criss-crossed by so many fine lines.

She could look at him now, as hard and as long as she wanted to, without the embarrassment of being caught doing so. And without worrying that by doing so she was giving him the vicarious pleasure of knowing that he still mattered to her. For he hadn't looked at her in ages, not even from the corner of his eyes. She always thought, and actually hoped, that she would catch him looking at her as just he had caught her doing so, many times. But he had continued to ignore her.

It was no different today, he was still ignoring her but in a completely different way.

Now he would never ever look at her. He would never love her, nor ever hate her. How then could she live on without all this; that which she had gotten so used to?

Sorrow finally crept up Chhaya'a guts and seized her throat and she let out a hoarse cry. Her eyes, finally moved by the sounds from her throat, started to shed tears. Tears that were so elated by the discovery of their own existence, that they continued to flow from strength to strength. Chhaya let out a long sigh of relief. At last, she had played out the last act in the drama of her life to absolute perfection.

15

Virginal Fantasy

Virginal Fantasy

Vaidehi lay on her side, her head resting on Mahesh's shoulder. Her forehead brushed against the stubble of his cheek. Every little while, his hand caressed the undulating curve of her hips, came up to her waist and rested there, as he drifted in and out of sleep. When she went back to lying on her back, his hand caressed the round of her breast and then came back to rest on her stomach. And this, after they had made glorious love twice over that night!

It was something he seemed to do almost every night since they had been married, as though to confirm the delicious reality of having his woman beside him all through the night. The pleasure of such a realisation was not his alone. Vaidehi, too, was delirious with happiness to be by his side. No amount of love-making was enough and she responded to his every touch, even when he had possibly done so subconsciously. Each caress would stir in her the delicious sensuousness of being a woman and she revelled in the sensation each time. It was a feeling so new and so exhilarating that she felt she could never ever have enough of it. Delirious and aroused, she felt that falling asleep would be a waste of time. Sometimes Vaidehi had to pinch herself to be certain she was his wife now. That in a primeval sort of way, she too possessed him, as much as he did her.

Mahesh was a fantastic lover — gentle and passionate at the same time. Of course, Vaidehi had known no other man to be able to really compare, but even then she instinctively knew that he was good. After all Mahesh had had plenty of experience with other women before he married her. He had been — to use his own words — 'an intellectual playboy' before matrimony. He had often in a most blasé manner, claimed to have lured the best of women onto many a bed or floor and on many a night or day, 'of their own volition'. Of course seeing her shocked and somewhat hurt face, Mahesh had promised her that all that had been a need and opportunity- based lifestyle, but with her entry into his life it would now be a thing of the past.

"A man has his needs — sometimes rather desperate needs — and in my position, there are always ways of fulfilling such needs quite easily. But I was very clear that when true love struck, lust would not be allowed to lead it," Mahesh had explained to Vaidehi, very early in their relationship. "And I think I was right, " he had continued, "for I finally did find you to love."

He had said the same thing to her again, a few hours ago. And Vaidehi had smiled to herself. It was good to feel that she was the *real* one. The one that he loved, and not merely lusted after. Although, Vaidehi had now realised that lust too was not such a bad thing after all!

Vaidehi smiled again at the memory of the first few days after marriage. She had been so gauche then. She did not know what went where or whether it was not a bit rude to keep her eyes and mouth closed as he kissed her all over. She used to look at him for approval all the time, and on one or two occasions she had even dared to ask whether she had passed muster. He usually always held on to her lovingly in the warm afterglow of lovemaking, sleepy and reluctant to talk. Frankly, she hadn't enjoyed sex the first few times. Much like the performance anxiety that men suffered from, Vaidehi suffered from response anxiety that was so typical of sexually inexperienced women.

Now, two months later, Vaidehi was so much more relaxed. In fact, she had began to feel absolutely magical sensations that she had never known had actually reposed in her own body. And the more she became alive and uninhibited about them, the more love and passion Mahesh had gradually infused into their lovemaking.

It seemed as if, in the last few weeks, Mahesh had been lying-in-wait waiting for her to develop a taste for, and then get addicted to, the passion that he realised he was capable of unleashing. Waiting perhaps for her to become as good as the lovers that he had known earlier.

It had been particularly beautiful today. For the first time, Vaidehi had unabashedly moaned with incredible pleasure for an eternity as they made love. Mahesh had been both amused and pleasantly surprised, and had declared that this time she had been like the ultimate fantasy come true for him.

At first, Vaidehi was happy to hear this. But later when she thought about it, she realised he had certainly borne her earlier inexperience with fond indulgence. Actually he had been quite reassured by it, for it proved to him beyond the faintest doubt that she was a virgin. He had never said so in as many words, but Vaidehi knew that this was what he was really thinking. And once she knew that he knew, she felt even more virtuous about it. Contrary to the modern pooh-poohing of the Indian belief that virginity was a gift to one's husband, she had come to believe that there wasn't a more accurate traditionally psychological theory that was as relevant now, as it must once have been.

To tell the truth, Vaidehi's 'gifted' virginity had been nothing but chance. Yet it had paid off handsomely for she wondered if she would have been as loved and cherished by Mahesh had she not been one.

"Isn't it true that you wanted a virgin as your bride though you yourself have made love to countless women?" Vaidehi asked.

It was not the first time she had asked him this question. Mahesh would always be a little irked each time. And to be fair to him, it was definitely an embarrassing question for any new husband to answer.

"They were not women I loved, but ones that I merely lusted for," he said rather emphatically as he first stroked her hair and then proceeded to play the drum on her cheek with his fingers. "You are the only one I love," he continued.

"You made love to them," she persisted. "After all, you cannot divorce feelings and emotions from the act of making love. Don't you feel love for me when you make love to me?" Vaidehi questioned, her eyes shining indignantly.

"Of course, I do. It's different with one's wife. But for a man, it is possible to just want to have sex with a woman without feeling any love for her. It's not like that for most women, therefore you will find it difficult to understand," he explained patiently, as if talking to a child.

"But those you made love to — they were also women, weren't they?" Vaidehi asked, very sure that he would have nothing to say to that.

"Yes, but you have no idea what kind of women those were. They were not at all like what you are," Mahesh said. "They were not real women. They were women who were out for a good time, as much as I was, with no feelings involved. Do you think I would hurt a real woman's feelings? Trust me, I can make out within the first few minutes that I spend with her what a woman is all about," he continued with supreme confidence.

"Does that mean that only virgins are real women?" she asked with persistence.

"No it doesn't mean that. A woman could lose her virginity

to a man she really loves, yet she may end up being someone else's wife. I don't say that that makes her a loose woman to her husband," Mahesh said weakly. "No, it certainly doesn't," he answered himself.

"Would you have fallen in love with me the same way if I had not been a virgin?" Vaidehi continued.

"Yes I think I would have. I certainly didn't check that fact with you when we were getting to know each other. But to tell you the truth I was quite sure that you were," he said in a voice that showed that he was clearly tiring. Somehow Mahesh never liked too much of this bare-my-soul-talk, Vaidehi had realised. And yet she just couldn't help but continue.

"I am sure that made you feel very good about me, didn't it?" she asked.

"Yes it did," Mahesh replied, a bit defiantly. "However much a man may pretend otherwise, he does feel great if his woman is untouched by another man. I was not hung up on virginity, but it certainly has its appeal. It always does to all men. Yet I'll say this much — that if everything else about you had been the same except your virginity, I would still have married you. I mean it. I think it is not just a question of virginity for its own sake. Virginity to me implies a complete innocence of body, soul and mind. I think when a woman loses her virginity, a little innocence of the other aspects goes too. And innocence is ultimately a woman's most beautiful jewel. So I am not sure that the rest of you would have been the same if you weren't a virgin," he said. He had been patient enough so far with all her questions. Now he was too exhausted to want to continue the discussion.

"Let's stop this pointless discussion now. What's important is what finally happened, and what finally is, between us.

Why bother about what might have been?" he said, as he turned on his side rubbing his legs against her thighs.

"Is this not beautiful enough?" he asked, turning back.

"It is," she sighed. But it was actually only half the truth.

Sometimes she thought that the problem with Mahesh was that he was much too honest. Most of the time he did not say right and comforting things that might be slightly untrue. But the flip side was that he could be trusted so completely about meaning exactly what he said. Oh how much she loved him! She knew that he was better than most Indian men, though not the ideal that any woman could ever hope for. He always said that he had a blazing temper, for one.

Vaidehi found that hard to believe as she had never seen it on display. But that, perhaps, was the source of his passion! He was immensely lovable—charming, successful, confident, and yet so very honest and simple at the core. Whatever he might say, Vaidehi was sure that the women he'd made love to, had really loved him, and had hoped he'd love them back. Little did they know of the theories of love and lust that roamed in his handsome head. Vaidehi was certain that for at least some of Mahesh's women, a hope for love was the moving spirit, and not the pure lust that he attributed to them.

But Vaidehi was a wife and she certainly had no sympathy for any of them. Oh how she hated the thought of those nameless, faceless women and the pleasures they had received from him! The pleasures they were rightfully only hers.

How dare Mahesh think that only a man wanted a wife untouched by another man! How she wished she could have him — untainted and virginal, as he had had her.

Mahesh laughed at the idea — that familiar indulgent, slightly mocking laugh. "But I never ever hid anything from you," he replied. "You knew all along about all these women, and the fact that I initiated all the encounters, with them playing willing partners. But that was all much before I met you. All of this has been over long since. It's simply not an issue anymore darling! Why is it disturbing you so much now? It's no reflection on you, you silly little girl," he said, ruffling her hair. "And now will you please let me get some sleep tonight?" he said in a tone of finality.

Vaidehi felt so angry. Here she was — a real woman alive with all the normal feelings of love, hate, possessiveness and jealousy. But Mahesh seemed he would never understand that she was neither silly, nor little, nor a girl anymore. Of course it was not possible for her to reverse his escapades but once, only once, did she want him to understand her feelings, no matter how absurd they sounded. They were born out of love for him — an aspect of physical love that she had discovered only when she had known his body. If he would merely realise that his past did hurt her and only once, just once, acknowledge that he did regret it, she was sure that it would assuage her restless feelings. She knew that Mahesh was sensitive and capable of doing that, if only he was ready to acknowledge that it was not abnormal for her to feel this way. Vaidehi decided just then, that she was somehow going to make him realise it.

There was only one way to do that. And it was to put him, for a brief while, in her shoes. Just to give him a taste of his own medicine, and to make him feel how the shoe pinched. Yes, that was now the only way!

"Mahesh," she whispered, and gently shook him from his sleep. "I have something to tell you," she said.

"Tomorrow," he mumbled, irritated.

"No Mahesh, I might not have the courage to tell you tomorrow. It's got to be now," she said in a tone of urgency.

He opened his eyes, his eyelids still weighed down with sleep. "What's the matter Vaidehi?" he asked.

"You have always been completely honest with me — even when the reality has been difficult for me to accept. I have admired you for that, and now I want to be as honest and truthful with you," said Vaidehi.

"Vaidehi, get to the point," Mahesh mumbled with irritation.

"First, promise me that you'll understand me in the same way as you have expected me to understand you," she asked.

"I promise, Vaidehi. Now go on," Mahesh said, by now, a trifle anxious.

"This is going to be fun," thought Vaidehi.

"I wasn't a virgin when I married you," she blurted.

"No, I promise you I had never been in love, it was only lust. And like you I was very clear that when love struck, lust would not be allowed to lead it. I was right wasn't I, for I found true love in you," Vaidehi whispered, her eyes downcast for a moment and then staring, unable to stop herself from looking at his face for his reaction. "You don't love me any less for it, do you?" she asked. "You said you wouldn't that day, do you remember?"

"Mahesh, are you listening," she repeated. "I just had to tell you someday, for you have been so completely honest with me. So I thought that I should be the same with you, shouldn't I? Mahesh? Are you listening? Mahesh?"

Vaidehi just could not make out what Mahesh was saying. Guttural sounds emanated from his throat as his Adam's apple bobbed up and down. His eyes were glazed. He drew his reddening face close to hers and held her jaws with both his hands in a pose that by now she had understood to be one prefacing a kiss on her lips. He looked strange and a little cockeyed as he brushed back the hair from the nape of her neck — what was going on? Was this some new form of foreplay? she wondered, a little overwhelmed at his raw passion at this most unexpected point of time.

"Mahesh... I love you," she whispered, as she shut her eyes, pleasantly reconciling herself to the lovemaking that she was sure was now going to follow a third time that night. She shut her eyes as she felt his kiss on her lips. Then she clasped his shoulders with her hands, and began making the circular movements on his back that he had taught her and which he loved so much. Her body throbbed, aching to be touched by him. Then suddenly, she felt his hands on both sides of her neck, pressing menacingly.

In a flash, her eyes opened registering what this was all really about. The blazing temper...

"Ma...aa....." she tried desperate but unable to speak, flaying her hands wildly as she felt herself choking and feeling a sharp piercing pain that shot upwards from her ears to her temples. The world swam around her.

Vaidehi attempted in vain to push Mahesh back. He threw her onto the bed with the strength of a giant and sat on her chest, his knees pinning down her arms on either side of her body as his fingers cut deeper and deeper into her neck.

A few rasps, a couple of gasps, and Vaidehi questioned no more...

16

Not Man Enough

Not Man Enough

PART 1

Babuji had just returned home. Devi spotted him through the jali as he walked across the veranda and towards the last room, where Mai usually sat at this time in the afternoon on her charpoy, with her knitting or crochet.

He looked ever so kind and handsome in his dusty - white kurta pajama. His grey sideburns shone with droplets of sweat and the greyish-green-moss-like stubble on his cheeks made him look a trifle sad and weary.

Devi ran across the inner rooms to reach Mai just as she got up in response to his knock.

"You've come back early," said Mai, declaring, more than really asking, the reason for this, for the downcast expression on his face was a clear indication of the story that was to follow.

"Tell Shakuntala to get some water and tell Kaka to make the tea to go with the *maththis*," Mai told Devi as she took the parcels that Babuji handed out.

Devi looked at Babuji's face. He smiled at her. She was relieved that he was not upset with her.

This was about the fourth time in the two years since her sister Vasanti's marriage, that her in-laws had summoned Babuji. The now sickening familiar routine had been laid out the very first time that he had been summoned. "Get your daughter to improve, or else take her back," Vasanti's mother-in-law had warned Babuji.

Babuji had stood there — a small man made smaller listening to the litany of complaints against his daughter. For, as they all pointed out, her misdemeanors were a reflection of her bad upbringing.

Of course they had a right to say anything they liked, Babuji had thought bitterly, his head bowed, not daring to exchange but a fleeting look at Vasanti, who had sobbed at this open humiliation of her father at her in-laws' hands.

A father of four daughters — what could he possibly do right anyway in this country? he had thought, while biting his lips as Vasanti's mother-in-law had gone on and on. And from the solemn expression that Devi saw on Babuji's face at this moment, she knew that it had probably been the same scenario this time around too.

PART 2

It was all because Vasanti — unlike her older sisters Riti and Babli, who had had their marriages arranged — had dared to fall in love. It was something that good girls simply did not do.

Brijesh's parents were unhappy at the fact that they had had no control over this most vital aspect of their son's life. Their logic was simple — a daughter-in-law who already had their son's affections would not feel the need to be good to others in the joint family in order to win it. Brijesh and Vasanti had tried to dispel these misgivings, but Vasanti's mother-in-law was never convinced. No matter what Vasanti did and how, her acerbic comments continued to flow like an unholy river.

Brijesh chose to remain the silent spectator. For, taking up for his wife would just mean adding fuel to the fire that already raged within his mother.

Poor Babuji had borne all this stoically — as stoically perhaps as he had borne the birth of one daughter after another, never failing in his love and duty towards them, even as Mai often openly cursed her fate. Riti, Babli, Vasanti — they were all married now, whether for better or for worse. Only Devi, all of fifteen years old, remained with them.

Somehow, Babuji's steadfast stoicism seemed to crumble only when the thought of this last one departing, just like her sisters after marriage, struck him. Although her birth was the final nail in the coffin of his hidden disappointment at never having a son, ironically she had brought him more joy than all the others put together. She had played cricket with him in the backyard, driven his tractor, kept his accounts and done all his banking errands ever since she was ten.

Devi had no time for trinkets. She loved to dress in the beige or brown trousers picked up from the streets of Jaipur by Babuji, which she wore with the loose, checked T-shirts brought in the smallest adult male size from the same markets. She had snipped her hair into a boyish cut and the only piece of jewellery she always wore were the two minimalist tiny gold dots in her ears.

Mai had always been irked by Devi's style of dressing and behaviour. She often commented that all this would be tolerable for just a little while more and that sooner, rather than later, Devi would have to become more feminine. Babuji of course would merely look on indulgently when Mai would start her tirade against Devi.

Devi thought nothing of rolling up her sleeves to fix a light bulb or of twisting an errant nut into submission. Once, she had even amazed her friend Deepti by picking up a dead lizard with her bare fingers. She had chucked it over the garden wall and Deepti had been so nauseous at the sight, that she had thrown up soon after.

When Deepti had regained her composure and appetite, she had of course been completely awed at her friend's courage and had related it to a proud Babuji.

Deepti always looked up to Devi. In Devi's presence Deepti felt ever so safe and protected. And Devi simply loved Deepti's wide-eyed innocence. She felt protective towards her. In these last few years they were such a together and a happy twosome that there was no place for a third other person in their circle of friendship.

Until recently, Mai used to tease them as "Mr & Mrs" whenever she saw their interaction and their vastly differing choice in clothes. But of late, she had stopped joking in this manner. It was clear that she did not find it amusing anymore.

Devi knew exactly why Mai had stopped joking about them. It was since Deepti, four years younger than her, had started menstruating, while Devi showed no such signs of impending womanhood. Even Devi's bustline had refused to emerge from her chest as though co-operating with her gender-defiant instincts.

"Just not sprouting," Mai would often comment as she poked Devi at her bustline. Your sisters were all fully developed by fifteen," she had often been remarking these days.

Devi would be irritated. "Is it my fault?" she would retort and then remove herself from the vicinity of Mai. She refused to brood about it. In fact in no way did she miss what Mai was missing for her. From Deepti's descriptions of the discomfort that the monthlies entailed, and her own memory of Babli's screams of pain when she had been in labour last year, womanhood in all its physical manifestations was hardly anything to look forward to.

Devi recalled the piles of stained sheets that had been brought out from Babli's hospital room after she had delivered her baby. She remembered Babli walking groggily into her room when she returned to their house. It had been the peak of the summer season those days, but the fan in Babli's room had never been allowed to go beyond its minimum speed. Babli's room had always been full with the smoke from the *dhoop* or the incense sticks constantly burning in one corner of the room. Beside Babli's bed had been kept a jug full of warm brown-coloured water. The water was bitter due to the *jeera* and *ajwain* that had been boiled in it. It was believed that these spices had beneficial properties for a nursing mother and her child.

Devi remembered Babli swathed in layers and layers of clothing, rivulets of sweat trickling down her neck. She had been so tired and uncomfortable on one particular day but one look at her husband Madhav who had come to visit her, and her eyes had shone. They were both so much in love with each other.

Before she could talk to him however, the womenfolk had led him away from the room, behaving as though she was in danger of being impregnated by him all over again, even if she merely had a conversation.

And in that stuffy room she had remained with her child throughout the customary forty-day period, secluded from most, and with minimal exposure to the elements both human and natural.

In those days Babli often thirsted for a cool drink of plain water but all she had been allowed was the black water with all its carminative properties that were supposed to do mother and child a world of good. Babli had confessed to Devi that she craved for normal food, but she was only given the lightest of yellow washed dal and jowari roti and a different variety of gourd each day, for it was believed that whatever the mother ate or drank, entered the infant through the milk from her breast. And so keeping the infant's tender systems in mind, the mother was to eat, drink and clothe herself in a way to minimise any danger to the baby. It was Babli's first big lesson in the selflessness which being a mother involved.

Devi remembered how she had once offered Babli cool water smuggled from the refrigerator, and Babli had given into the temptation, confessing to Devi as she drank it that she had felt satiated for the first time in many weeks that day.

But all hell had broken loose the next day as *munna* had come down with a cold. Their secret was found out and Mai had duly chastised Devi. For Babli, the trauma of seeing her child suffer because of her indulgençe was punishment enough, and was a lesson learnt for life.

After a few days, Babli had left for her husband's house. She had looked resplendent, and had been glowing at the prospect of finally being allowed to stand next to Madhav, their eyes twinkling with the magic of love and happy parenthood.

Devi wondered if she could ever feel that way about any man; as her sisters did. She hated looking at men's pictures. She even detested the posters of film heroes that Deepti, like the other girls in her class, put up in their rooms or pasted on the inner walls of their cupboards. In fact what she did enjoy, was looking at girls. She loved staring at the beautiful curvature of their bodies, and their colourful clothes. This was however not a love of wanting to be like them — it was more as Devi had started admitting to herself lately of wanting to love them. She wanted to hold, feel, caress and kiss them; feelings that only a man was supposed to feel.

Devi had confessed this to Deepti and Deepti had told Devi, that no matter what she felt was right or wrong in the eyes of the world, Deepti would always love her for what she was. Deepti had then held Devi's hands and placed them over her tender budding breasts and then shut her eyes with mysterious pleasure. Devi too had felt a strange pleasure deep in her innards, as she touched and caressed Deepti and had ached to, but resisted, touching her more.

Devi shared these feelings with Deepti now, as she had shared everything else in the past with Deepti — feelings both moral and immoral, named and unnamed.

And now, she shared a brand new secret with her. It was perhaps a really wild dream. But also one which had the potential of exploding into fantastic reality if the words of the story that Devi had read so many times in these last two days were indeed true.

It was Deepti who had read this story first. It was an article in *Today's Woman* magazine published from Bombay which profiled a sixteen-year-old girl whose story read just like Devi's. It was the story of a girl who had felt like a boy trapped in a girl's reluctant body and whose battle to come to terms with her strangeness had had a fairy-tale ending. The girl had undergone a series of sex-change operations to finally emerge as a boy. Lalita had turned into Lalit and was blissfully happy at last.

Devi's heart had pounded the first time she read the story. And it continued to pound with no less force, everytime she did. Thereafter it almost burst out of her chest when Deepti goaded her to emulate Lalita and even promised that she would marry her 'when' (not just if) she became a man. Her chances of being allowed the operations were high, as Deepti explained. She had not started menstruating and, like Lalita she would surely score full marks in the psychological tests that the doctors would conduct before they consented to do the operations. Devi was already so completely manly.

For Devi, Deepti was proving to be a real soulmate — she was giving words to Devi's forbidden dreams and bringing them into the realm of the possible. She was daring her to dream, what could be a dream come true for both of them.

If Lalita could become Lalit, surely Devi could turn into Dev! For the first time in all these years, Deepti was taking the lead in their friendship; as if there was truly as much in this for her, as there was for Devi. Devi saw how Deepti suddenly seemed so mature, and aware, so intelligent and practical. If it hadn't been for Devi and the words that she had used to tell Babuji this dream, they would never have been able to even discuss such a contentious issue with her father.

At first Babuji had been incensed, then he had turned a little amused. A little later he had muttered, completely mesmerised by his own thoughts, "Dev... Dev... Dev... ?" He had smiled such a strange and beautiful smile that moment. Yet it had taken many such rounds of convincing before Babuji had finally consented to give this fantastic idea a serious thought. And think it over he certainly did. Deep in his heart he knew that he would not be able to take the eventual departure of Devi as stoically as he had been able to take his other daughters' adieus. Perhaps this was his last chance; in fact his only chance to keep her with him forever.

So many wonderful things were possible and were happening in the modern world, he thought. This was one of them. But then again, Babuji would think of the ancestral wisdom which he had been brought up with and which simply advised that one must never tamper with nature. And playing with nature was exactly what this sex-change was going to involve.

Devi and Deepti could sense that Babuji was wavering. They were emboldened by this wavering, which was all too apparent on his transparent face, and pestered him over and over again. In the end, Babuji had somewhat serious-facedly admitted that he was finally feeling positive about the whole issue. He said that he would consider finding out a little more about the possibilities of Devi's transformation. It was however at this time that he had received the summons from Vasanti didi's in-laws and the issue had therefore taken a backseat. Of course they all decided that Mai was not to be told anything right now, knowing her propensity to chest-beat and overreact under stressful circumstances.

PART 3

Babuji sipped his tea, lost in thought, not once looking at his favourite snack of *maththis* that Mai had put on the table in front of him. Deep furrows of thought had appeared on his forehead. Devi remembered her mother's favourite piece of advice that she had given to each of her sisters before they were married, as she now looked at her father's face.

Mai had told each one of her daughters as they had left home "There is a secret way in which to get your way with a man — any man. If you can judge which is the right moment to approach him with a request, and which is the moment to retreat into silence, you will have conquered the world."

The world! — the woman's world that is — the territory that lay enclosed within the perimeter of her home. Of course right now Devi was going to heed this piece of sane advice, as she did not intend disturbing Babuji with anything controversial. And so she waited patiently and quietly in a corner of the room, not venturing to ask him whether he had made up his mind to take her to the sex-change doctor they had read about in Bombay.

But Mai knew that Babuji needed to talk, as much as they needed to know what had happened today at Vasanti's house. He related it all wearily — the cold reception he received from her father-in-law and the sorrow in the fact that Brijesh's eyes had not met his even once. Vasanti's mother-in-law had beat her chest and wailed about what havoc his daughter had created in their family. But what had affected Babuji more than all this, he said, was Vasanti sobbing and gritting her teeth as she heard it all silently.

"My poor daughter!" he had thought, his heart crying for her.

"What else can a woman do but cry and bear it?" said Mai bitterly. "After all, she has to live there all her life. She is supposed to enter her in-laws' house in a *doli* and leave it only in her *arthi*."

"That's how our people, that's how our society has chosen to have it. It doesn't really have to be like that. I would like Vasanti and all my daughters to know if they are ever in need or in trouble, they have their father's house to come back to," said Babuji softly. Brave words indeed, that swelled Devi's heart with pride.

"It's all very well to say that but think of the long run. How long will her father and mother be around to look after her if a daughter were to return. In our household there are no brothers to take care of them — can a daughter eventually live alone here even if she were to return from her marital home?" asked Mai with a sigh. It was a familiar sigh — a burden-of-four-daughters sigh. "If only God had given me one just one son," she continued.

Then, looking rather oddly at Babuji she added, "If only *you* had given me one, just one son!"

How foolish of Mai to have said that! And what bad timing! thought a shocked Devi as she watched Babuji's face stiffen at her words. They all knew enough of biology by now to understand the gravity of what Mai had known for long but had spoken about only today.

Her words had hurt Babuji and it showed on his face. He looked at her with an uncharacteristic eye.

"Maybe I can still give you a son," said Babuji, as Mai now looked at him with embarrassed disbelief. But only Devi, from her corner of the room knew the exact import of what Babuji had just said.

Babuji got up and walked away — a confident not tired walk. As he passed Devi and she looked up at him, he caressed her head and then held up her chin. "I will take you to Bombay. Get ready to leave tomorrow morning," he said smiling. "Now I will do all that I can to fulfill your fantasy — our fantasy." Devi's elation knew no bounds, but she took care to suppress its expression.

She spent all evening packing her suitcases with Deepti, sharing their future dreams with her. Mai had not the faintest idea of the mission of this trip, and neither Deepti nor Devi could bring themselves to tell her anything about it. Babuji promised them that he would tell her in course of time, when he felt the time was right and when they themselves were sure of what really was possible in their plan.

The next morning, Babuji finished his bath and his prayers. He had thought that he would be nervous but was overwhelmed by his own sense of calm.

He looked at his watch. It showed 7:30 a.m. Mai was praying in the aangan. He had not told her anything about the real mission of this trip and had simply said that he and his favourite daughter Devi had planned a week's holiday in Bombay. Mai had found this odd but she did not suspect anything; at least nothing as bizarre as the reality.

Babuji came out of his room. He stood outside Devi's bedroom door, surprised that there were no sounds from inside. He had fixed her alarm last night for 6:30 a.m. and she was usually one to be ready very promptly. He smiled at the thought that she had probably been too excited last night to have slept on time. She might have switched off the alarm and gone right back to sleep when it rang.

He knocked at her door once and then a second time, Then, a little alarmed he knocked almost repeatedly. There was still no response. Babuji pushed the door gently.

A hoarse scream escaped his throat. There was Devi, hanging from the ceiling fan dressed most unlike herself in a ghagra choli. A thousand screams joined into a long wail as Babuji cried out in shock. Devi! Why? Why Devi? Babuji screamed again and again, completely unable to comprehend what he was seeing.

And then Babuji's eyes fell on Devi's favourite pair of beige trousers, the one she had been wearing the previous evening. There they lay on the ground, the crotch still damp with a maroon patch of menstrual blood.

41-D